The Death of Big Butch

LARRY SCEURMAN

The Death of Big Butch
Copyright pending 2022 by Larry Sceurman
ISBN: 978-1-957863-03-0

Published by Parisian Phoenix Publishing, Easton, Pennsylvania USA

Front cover image: Joan Zachary, joanzachary.com
Back cover images: Jennie E. Hannis; Cottonwood Studio/pexels.com
Author photo: Barbara Sceurman
Special Thanks: Maryann Ignatz and Steve's Cafe, Phillipsburg, N.J.; Eva Parry

C O N N E C T with the publisher:
ParisianPhoenix
ParisBirdBooks

C O N N E C T with the author:
lvstorytelling.org/live/teller/larry-sceurman/
larbarstory@gmail.com

DEDICATION

To my lovely and beautiful wife, Barbara,
for all her support and encouragement

Tuesday, May 21, 1974

I t's a beautiful spring evening and the sun leaves pinkish-orange streaks across the western sky. A vintage burgundy '65 Mustang rolls to a stop. Sally sits pressed against the steering wheel, the bulk of her body preventing her from reaching the door handle.

Jimmy exhales, fearing that Sally will scrape the tires against the curb. He hates sitting in the passenger seat and having Sally drive.

Sally turns to Jimmy. "Open the door for me and get me out of this thing."

Jimmy runs to the driver's side of the car and opens the door.

"Sal, this is not a thing. It's a 1965 Mustang fastback 2+2 with pony interior."

Sally extends her arm for Jimmy to help her out.

"I know it's a '65 Mustang 2+2, and that it's hard to get out of. Someday it may be worth more than what you paid for it," she says tersely, repeating verbatim the points he has made in the past. "But when you feel like you're freakin' 52 months pregnant and stuck behind the steering wheel and you have to get out of this bucket seat, it's a thing. I don't know why we can't have a regular four-door car… It would make our life simpler."

Jimmy sighs.

"What, are you kidding me? I'm not driving around in a four-door family delight."

Sally gets on her feet, steps to the sidewalk, and turns to Jimmy with her hands on her hips.

"Jimmy, just what the hell do you think we are?"

She gestures toward the back seat. "There's Little Jimmy sleeping in his car seat, the trunk and the back seat are full of groceries and my belly sticks out like I ate a basketball… because I'm pregnant. We have a two-year-old child and we're going to have another child, that's a freakin' family, Jimmy."

She raises her voice, not enough to wake their son, Little Jimmy, but enough to emphasize her point.

"Remember I'm the one that does the driving in this family. You lost your driver's license because you drive drunk. Cars and drinking don't really help family life."

Jimmy throws up his hands and with a little shake of his head says, "Okay, okay. Do you want me to get Little Jimmy out of the car seat?"

Sally rolls her eyes. "Yes, Jimmy. If we had a four-door car or a little station wagon, I could get him in and out of the car myself."

Jimmy looks at Sally's angelic face, framed by her dark brown hair, and stares into her whiskey-colored eyes, full of the intensity of the irritation she has toward him. He hesitates, knowing he should keep his mouth shut… but there is this sixteen-year-old motor-head that still lingers in Jimmy's soul. If your car isn't cool, neither are you.

Out it comes. He can't stop it.

"No way. No station wagons," Jimmy says. "I sold the '60 'Vette to put aluminum siding on the house! What the hell more do you want?"

"I want a station wagon and a husband that is not a drunk."

Jimmy looks at Sally for a moment and without a word, he reaches into the back seat, unbuckles Little Jimmy, and lifts him out. His whole demeanor changes and his voice is kind and soothing.

"Hey, sleepyhead, we're home now."

Jimmy kisses the boy on the cheek. Sally takes Jimmy's lead and her sharp words dull to a gentler tone.

"I'll open the trunk and bring in a bag of groceries," she says.

Jimmy gives her a peace-for-now look, saying, "Don't hurt yourself."

Sally looks back with what he considers her sneering smile.

"Take Little Jimmy upstairs," she says. "I'll come up and get him ready for bed."

While Sally puts Little Jimmy to bed, Jimmy brings the rest of the groceries in and starts putting them away when the phone rings. He recognizes the voice on the other end of the line.

"Oh, hi, George," he says.

Jimmy and George have been best friends since kindergarten. They did everything together. They went to school together. They went into the Army together. They were the best man at each other's wedding. They are godfathers to each other's sons. But they are also quite different. Jimmy has a darker complexion with thick deep brown hair. He is much more outgoing, a little loud, and humorous. George has light curly hair and is fair-skinned. He is quiet, a thinker, and not as spontaneous. But they always got along, not a cruel or unkind word was ever spoken between them. Not even when their disagreements turned angry.

Sally walks into the kitchen.

"Who's on the phone?" she asks.

Jimmy puts his hand over the phone and says, "It's George," and quickly returns to the phone conversation.

"So, what's up?" Jimmy says. "Bad news? What do you mean, bad news?"

Suddenly, Jimmy no longer hears. He only reacts.

"Holy shit, you got to be fucking kidding me…How? Oh, my God, I just can't believe it."

Sally tugs on his shirt. "What? What? Jimmy, what's wrong?

Jimmy turns to Sally, confused, "Big Butch died. Heart attack."

Sally yells, "Oh, my God!"

She puts her hand over her mouth and drops onto the kitchen chair. Jimmy continues his phone conversation.

"How in the hell could he have a heart attack? He's only twenty-seven years old…Really, no shit…Yeah, he was a big man…Well, I just can't believe it! Big Butch is dead. Holy shit. When? Okay, Friday night at seven. Collins' funeral home…Yeah, we'll go together. Sally or I will give you a call…Hey, how are Butch's Mom and Pop? I guess they are…Okay, thanks for calling. We'll see you, bye."

Jimmy hangs up the phone and turns to Sally, "I just can't believe it. Big Butch and only twenty-seven years old."

"Just what the hell happened?" Sally asks.

"Heart attack. He came in from cutting the grass, sat down at the kitchen table, started to drink a beer—and he died."

Jimmy sits at the kitchen table next to Sally. He takes a deep breath and exhaling, he lowers his head and then turns slowly to Sally. He has tears in his eyes so she takes his hand, leaning over and kissing him softly on the cheek.

Tears flow and in a soft voice, trying to push down the lump in his throat, Jimmy says, "Big Butch was such a nice guy. He was a really good guy. I can't believe he's gone."

Sally slowly takes a beer out of the refrigerator, opens it, and pours it into two glasses, a very small amount for herself. She sits down next to Jimmy, slides his beer over to him, and then raises her glass. Jimmy picks up his glass, touching the edge of Sally's. Clink.

They both say, "To Big Butch."

"One hell of a good guy," Jimmy adds.

Later that night in the spoon position, Sally's butt to Jimmy's belly, he reaches over and puts his hand on her pregnant belly. With a little pat, he says, "I can feel the baby. Do you feel that?"

"Yes. The baby is quite active tonight. I think it's going to be soon."

Jimmy gets up on one elbow. He leans toward Sally.

"Not tonight," he says, "You mean a couple of days?"

"I mean about a week or so."

They settle to their original positions. Even though they cannot see each other's faces, Jimmy knows Sally is smiling. So is he.

Then, Sally asks, "Hey, what was Big Butch's real name? I never knew it."

Jimmy chuckles.

"Ralph. Ralph Franklin Donchez. You never knew his real name?"

"No. I only ever knew him as Big Butch."

"That's funny."

Jimmy rubs her belly, then he moves her shiny dark brown hair and kisses her softly on her neck. Moving his hands slowly back to her belly, he says quietly, "Here we are. Twenty-six years old, having our second child. We have a house, work is good, and our biggest problem is, should we buy a four-door car?"

He pauses.

"Then, you get the news that one of your very best friends just dropped dead. Right now, I have my hand on a life that will come out and meet the world in a week or so. It's like the cycle of life… birth and death."

Sally lifts Jimmy's hand from her belly and kisses it. "Go to sleep, you have a busy day tomorrow. I love you."

She kisses his hand once more, then puts it back on her belly.

"I love you, too," says Jimmy.

He falls asleep with his hand on life and his head full of death.

Wednesday, May 22, 1974

The next morning, Jimmy shuffles into the kitchen. He gives Sally a kiss, grabs a cup of coffee off the counter, and slides into his seat at the kitchen table next to Little Jimmy in his highchair.

"Hey, there, little tadpole! What's that you're eating?"

Little Jimmy says, "Daddy. Cheerios. Banana."

He extends his arm toward Jimmy with Cheerios stuck on his fingers and says, "Eat, Daddy."

Jimmy takes the toddler's hand, puts it in his mouth, and makes believe he's eating Little Jimmy's fingers. Little Jimmy pulls his fingers out, the Cheerios gone.

"Yum, yum, good fingers," Jimmy says.

Little Jimmy giggles, picks up some more Cheerios and sticks out his hand. "More."

Sally, in her pink bathrobe, sits across the table. She has a little smile of contentment on her face and a cup of coffee in her hand. Her smile fades.

"I still can't get over Big Butch."

Jimmy nods. "Me too. It's as if it didn't happen."

"George said Friday night at Collins', right?" Sally says.

"Yeah, that's what he said."

Jimmy doesn't want to talk about Big Butch. Sally must sense it because she changes the subject. She asks Jimmy about work, about how busy a day he'll have.

"Well, I have to finish detailing the '56 Chevy so the customer can pick it up. That'll give us more room to work on the '38 Buick Roadmaster. Jack wants to put the transmission in the Buick today. I know he can't do it by himself, so I'll be helping him with that."

Jimmy thinks for a minute.

"Sal, you got to come over today and check out this Buick. It's really nice. It's a '38 Buick Roadmaster model 81 Touring Sedan, which means it has all the goodies on it. Dual side-mount fender wheel wells, a Buick Dynaflash straight eight engine, radio, the speedometer goes up to 120, and a lot of neat chrome goodies on it."

"You really do like working on them old cars with your Uncle Jack," she says. "You never did care about working at Mack Truck or The Steel, even though you would make more money and we would have better benefits."

"Oh, come on, Sal," he says. "Could you see me doing the same thing day after day, punching a clock and taking orders from some boss with his head up his ass?"

"I'm just saying, Jimmy."

Sally walks to the stove.

"You want eggs, cereal?" she asks.

"Cereal. Raisin bran and peanut butter toast," Jimmy says.

Sally puts bread in the toaster.

"But what about the benefits?" she says again, reviving the previous conversation. "You know… with two kids now and all."

"Sally, don't start this again. Our insurance benefits are okay. They'll pay for most of the new baby's hospital bills."

"But we're paying for them, we have a monthly bill," Sally explains. "At Mack or The Steel, the company pays for the benefits."

She places his cereal bowl on the table.

"Here's your raisin bran."

Jimmy starts to eat. Nothing more is said between them. The only conversation is with Little Jimmy about colors and food that he likes. Jimmy moves to the chair by the door and reaches for his work boots.

"Look at Big Butch," Jimmy says. "He worked in the office at the steel company and it was okay for him. He liked it, I guess. He didn't say much about it. It was just a fucking job."

"Your language, Jimmy," Sally says.

"Your language, Jimmy," Little Jimmy repeats.

"Sorry," Jimmy says.

He shoves one foot in a boot.

"But you know what I mean. It was just a job to Big Butch. He liked it, he was glad he had it, it was just a job."

He laces his other boot.

"But what I do is different," he says. "It's special for me. It's creative. Not just anybody can paint a car like I do. And every day there is a challenge, every day you can do something exceptional, not just half-assed."

Sally goes over and kisses Jimmy on the cheek.

"I know you're a really good painter and you are a really good provider, too," she says. "I'm glad you're doing what you love to do. I just get scared sometimes. But a little station wagon would be handy. Isn't the '38 Buick a four-door?"

"Four-door," Little Jimmy repeats.

"Yes," Jimmy confirms.

He pauses for a moment as he looks into Sally's fox-like brown eyes. Then, he stands and pulls her closer. She gives him her playful smile.

"You wouldn't like the Buick," he says, "because the rear doors are what they call 'suicide doors.' They open the opposite way with the hinges on the back of the door. They're not childproof."

He gives her a long, love-filled kiss and laughs.

"Sal, you are one manipulating lady, but you're my foxy lady," he says. "No station wagon."

He goes to Little Jimmy, gives him a kiss, and heads out the door.

Standing at the kitchen sink, she stares out the window. Her thoughts swirl in her mind. She sees herself screaming at a drunken Jimmy. Sally does like the fact that Jimmy works with his Uncle Jack and that they restore classic cars. She likes the idea of the family business and that they only live a half a block from the garage. She knows that Jimmy is proud of being part of the family tradition, yet she worries.

"I know things will be all right," she says out loud. "I got to trust him. But sometimes, I just can't."

The garage, Jack's Restoration, was started by Jimmy's grandfather Pappy Jack, Uncle Jack's father, but it was just a hobby then. Uncle Jack built it into a lucrative business. Pappy Jack still comes around about once a week. Sometimes he does a little work, but mostly he kibitzes with the older neighbors. The whole situation is unique. Jack's Restoration is an oversized three-bay garage located in an alley, half a block off the main drag. Uncle Jack lives in the house near the garage, the house that he grew up in, and Jimmy and Sally live down the street.

When Jimmy gets to the garage, he tells Uncle Jack about Big Butch's death. Jack knew Big Butch but not that well. He lets Jimmy go on talking about Big Butch and how great a guy he was and how he just can't believe it and puff, he's gone.

Jack puts the Buick on the lift and in the air. He rolls a toolbox into place and starts to take out the appropriate tools, laying them on top of the box. The whole time Jimmy's still talking about death and Big Butch.

"Jimmy, I need your help," Jack says. "Let's put this tranny in and then you can finish up the '56 Chevy."

That is the start of the workday.

Uncle Jack is Jimmy's mother's brother, a tall, quiet man with strong hands and arms and a strong personality. He is the type of guy who has a presence about him; you know he is in the room even if he doesn't say a word. If you ask Jimmy what he really liked about Uncle Jack, he would say without hesitation that he's a great teacher and has a strange sense of humor that makes you think.

About 2 o'clock that afternoon, Jimmy finishes putting a coat of primer on the rear fenders of the Buick and yells to Jack, "I'm goin' up the street to get a pack of smokes."

They both know that Jimmy's going to rifle down a couple of beers at Bucky's Place with old Stanley.

"Okay," Jack says, "but don't be too long,"

As Jimmy is walking up the hill to Main Street, thoughts of Big Butch slip into his mind. Why Big Butch? And why was he taken at twenty-seven? Jimmy slows his pace, the memory of going to the 1964 New York World's Fair with Big Butch coming into view which makes him smile.

He crosses Main Street and pushes the door open under the sign Stanley's Cleaners. The bell above the door jingles.

"Hey! You ready for a little refreshment?" Jimmy asks.

He bangs on the counter.

"Come on, you old geezer! I've been standing here for fifteen minutes."

Stanley looks up from the sewing machine.

"Oh, Jimmy," he says. "How long have you been standing there?"

"Fifteen minutes," Jimmy answers.

"Oh, you have not."

Stanley gets up from the sewing machine, takes off his apron, and puts his glasses in his pocket.

"I'll be with you in a minute," he says.

Stanley stretches his back by twisting it a little bit and starts to walk stiffly toward the counter, his eyes on Jimmy.

"I got what you call geriatric inertia," he explains. "What's at rest wants to stay at rest, and what's in motion would rather be at rest."

Jimmy laughs.

"There's no rush Stanley. The beer will still be cold."

The two of them stand on the curb. As soon as he sees a break in the traffic, Jimmy runs into the middle of the street and stands with his arms stretched like a self-appointed crossing guard. As Stanley crosses the street, Jimmy calls out like a sarcastic cheerleader.

"Come on Stanley, you can do it," he yells. "Don't give up now! That's right, one foot in front of the other! Oh, you're almost there, you old S.O.B.! Yay, you made it!"

Stanley steps onto the sidewalk. He turns to Jimmy.

"You're the son of a bitch, wise guy."

But there is laughter in Stanley's voice. The two stroll into Bucky's place, Stanley with a smile on his face and Jimmy with the posture of a man with a purpose. They park themselves on the barstools at their usual spot by the front door, so they can see who is coming or going and react with the appropriate greeting or snide comment. Haas the Bartender refers to them as "the peanut gallery."

Stanley and Jimmy are the most unlikely barroom buddies that you will ever see. At twenty-six-years old, about six foot tall, and medium built, Jimmy is a blue-collar type of guy, with a big, dark handlebar mustache and long sideburns. An old striped railroad work cap sits on his longish, dark brown hair. A denim work shirt, jeans, and work boots are his everyday dress.

Stanley's pushing eighty. He stands a few inches shorter than Jimmy, but in his youth, they might have been the same. Now, Stanley has a soft pudginess. His egg-shaped head is accented by baldness and a broad smile. He has an Ed Wynn voice and a contagious, musical laugh. He always wears a sport shirt and khaki slacks (that he calls "chinos"), both nicely-pressed, and highly-shined loafers with socks that match the color of his shirt. Today they are blue. The one thing the men have in common is that they wear suspenders.

Haas puts two glasses of Miller draft in front of them.

"Well, if it isn't the old barroom philosopher and the young hippie mechanic," the bartender says.

Haas has been tending bar at Bucky's for the past twenty years, ever since Bucky bought it in 1954. He's as much of a fixture as the carved wooden animals and the stained-glass frames around the mirrors of the back bar. Even though Bucky's place has evolved into a friendly neighborhood bar, it still has the grand feel and looks of a 1920s hotel.

The bar is long with the beer taps and cash register located in the middle. Wooden stools with red Naugahyde seats, smooth and worn, stand on the wooden floor, slightly grooved by years of use. Across from the bar are wooden booths, also worn and smooth with age. You might say that the smell of smoke, stale beer, and furniture polish add to the atmosphere.

Haas adds to the mood with his gruff voice and no-nonsense look. He's medium height and build with a gray crew cut, a face like a Boston Terrier, and always, a bow-tie.

Stanley taps his money on the bar.

"Haasie, take that out of here and one for yourself," he says.

Haas takes the money and then looks at Jimmy.

"You better behave yourself. Bucky bought some used tape record-ers from the White House, real cheap. It was a President Nixon Sale. Now he's placing microphones under the bar."

Stanley and Jimmy laugh.

Then, Jimmy remarks, "I always knew Bucky was a Republican."

They sip their beer. Stanley turns to Jimmy.

"So how is the world of Jimmy today?"

"One of my best friends died yesterday," he answers. "You remember Big Butch? Used to come in the Fire Hall with me from time to time."

Stanley offers a look of concern.

"Oh, yes, that big fellow," Stanley says. "What happened?"

"Heart attack," Jimmy says. "He came in from cutting the grass, sat down, opened a beer, and bang! He was dead. I don't understand it. Twenty-seven years old."

"That's a shame," says Stanley. "Sorry to hear that."

Stanley then takes a sip of his beer and stares at the glass.

"Death doesn't have to make sense," he says. "When you get to be my age, death can become an old friend that takes you to the next part of your journey."

He pauses, fingers clasping the beer tightly before releasing it completely.

"But when you're young, death is foolish," Stanley continues. "I remember when I was in France during World War I. I was in the balloon corps. You know, observation balloons. I drove truck for the ground support team. Every day I would see these young lieutenants go thousands of feet up in the air in just a wicker basket and risk their lives. But the only casualties that I saw were by artillery fire that hit our camp and it was just sheer luck that you got through it. I saw the young boys that died. I put their bodies onto stretchers and haul them away. They were gallant young men for just being there and death seemed honorable."

Jimmy thinks for a minute.

"I understand that," he says. "I experienced that part of combat in 'Nam. This is different."

Stanley nods. "But when a young person dies and there's no rhyme or reason to it, it stirs up all kinds of emotions. You feel sad, angry, and doubtful. There's a distrust with God. You have a chaos of emotions, which leaves you with the question, why? Even more so than on the battlefield."

Jimmy stares at Stanley.

"Man, ain't that the truth. Stanley, that is some heavy shit, that's more than being a barroom philosopher," he says. "What was it you said? 'Chaos of emotions, which leaves you with the question…Why?' That is exactly how I feel. I'm all fucked up inside and it always comes to the question, why? So why is that?"

Stanley smiles.

"Part of it is because you're young. When you're young, you're much more frightened of death. That's just the way it is," Stanley tells him. "We realize that we can die, too, and that death could be just around the corner. Then, one day, we find out that the secret of life is death."

Jimmy looks right at Stanley.

"Some more heavy shit," he says, "but I guess you're right."

He lights a smoke and waves to Haas.

"Haasie! Give us two more and two shots of Imperial."

Haas nods and turns to get the bottle.

"Watch me wind up Haasie," Jimmy murmurs to Stanley.

"Okay, boys, a buck fifty," Haasie says.

He pours the shots.

"Take it out of here," Jimmy says, tapping the money on the bar in front of his glass.

"Hey, Haasie, I hear they're putting in a bar at the mall," Jimmy says. "A discotheque called the White Hills Society."

"Screw that," says Haas. "It won't hurt us. I hope they go belly up."

Jimmy sips his beer.

"It's progress, Haasie," he says. "It's 1974. We need a change in White Hills."

"Change. The Hell with change. This is the last generation that will live in this village in some kind of normal life," Haas spouts. "The Mall, the fuckin' White Hills Mall is the… what's the word they use for this shit? Icon. That's the word. The icon of White Hills Township is now the White Hills Mall."

Haas wipes the bar in front of Stanley and Jimmy. Stanley sits with his arms folded. Jimmy strokes his mustache.

"What a bunch of shit!" Haas continues. "It's not for us in the little villages that make up the Township. Here in Weissberg, there's everything you need. There's Ernie's market a grocery store, two drugstores, Lucy's Light Lunch, Junior's Doggie Shop, three gas stations, one with a luncheonette, a hardware store, a barbershop, post office, dry cleaners, and tailor shop, a shoemaker, two little corner stores, Greenawalt's and Snookie's Corner."

Haas pauses, because he is running out of breath and his face turns dark red.

"Two barrooms, the White Hills Hotel and us, plus the Weissberg Fire Hall and the American Legion. Who needs this goddamn mall with a discotheque?" he says. "It's the death of the township. It's killing our way of life! We'll become a traffic jam, and parking lots, and end up like the suburbs of fucking New Jersey with more crime and less values. I'm telling you this mall is a bad thing. Soon White Hills as we know it will be dead."

Haas takes the money and walks away. Stanley leans toward Jimmy.

"You're bad. Jimmy, sometimes you're no damn good."

"He loves it," says Jimmy. "That's part of his job, being a contrary, old prick. But he does have a point. I don't know if this big mall is good or bad, but things are starting to change. And with change, there is an end to things. It's like something must die for something to grow… I wonder why Big Butch had to die."

Jimmy raises a shot glass toward Stanley and Stanley does the same to Jimmy.

"Here's to Big Butch," says Jimmy.

"Here, here," Stanley says.

They down their shots and both take a sip of beer. Stanley nods to Jimmy in a gesture that ordains the toast and what Jimmy had said.

"I should get going," Jimmy says.

He takes two big gulps of beer and puts his cigarette out in the ashtray.

"I got to get back to Jack and remove more chrome parts and running boards. Oh, Stanley, you got to stop at the garage and see this great '38 Buick. It looks like a freakin' Eliot Ness car."

Stanley smiles with his biggest grin.

"I have fond memories of a '38 Buick."

Jimmy laughs. "I bet you do."

He rises from the barstool and pats Stanley on the back. Then, he looks over to Haas, giving him a salute while saying thanks. Jimmy turns and walks toward the door.

"Say hello to Uncle Jack," Stanley calls out as a final farewell.

Jimmy walks down the hill toward the garage. His mind flows with memories of Big Butch.

He remembers the after-school pinochle games at Big Butch's house. Sometimes there were eight or ten guys hanging out there, but there were always at least four guys to get a pinochle game going. Big Butch was the primo pinochle player. His thoughts go back to sitting at the table playing cards, drinking soda, smoking cigarettes, and eating Mr. Donchez's chocolate Tastykake cupcakes.

Jimmy laughs aloud as he walks down the hill, thinking how pissed off Mr. Donchez would get when there were no more Tastykakes for his lunch.

Jimmy enters the garage and sees Sally standing beside the Buick.

"Hi, honey. Where's Little Jimmy?" he asks.

"Hi, Daddy! Driving a car."

Jimmy looks in the old Buick. Little Jimmy stands on the seat behind the steering wheel, and Uncle Jack stands outside the car by the driver's door.

"Wow. What a big boy you are," says Jimmy. "You having fun?"

"Yes," Little Jimmy says with a laugh.

Jimmy walks to Sally and gives her a kiss.

"A beer and whiskey kiss," Sally says with her sneering smile. "Been at Bucky's Place having a few with old Stanley."

"She got you Jimmy, no way to wiggle out," Uncle Jack calls from the other side of the Buick.

"I was only there for two beers," Jimmy says. "So, Sal, what do you think of this old Buick? She'll be really something when she's done."

Jimmy changes the subject because he doesn't want to be lectured on his drinking and Sally knows this. Sally knows that the death of Big

Butch is on his mind and that he must deal with it in his own way. She knows that Jimmy is foolish with his emotions, but Sally is wise enough to give him space and to love him in his space.

"George called," says Sally. "He wants to know if you are going to the Crazy Horse tonight and if you are, he can pick you up at 7:30."

Jimmy looks at Sally and nods okay. He goes to Little Jimmy.

"Well…Are you going or not?" asks Sally.

Jimmy scoops Little Jimmy into his arms and walks to Sally. Speaking softly to Sally, Jimmy urges her to step outside the garage so Uncle Jack can't hear them. When outside, Jimmy stands close to Sally with Little Jimmy still in his arms. He looks into Sally's eyes with his "I'll be a good boy" face.

He speaks clearly and almost calculating, as if what he is saying has been rehearsed. Sally stops him in mid-sentence.

"Okay, Jimmy," she relents.

He stands confused. His emotions recoil. The little speech he rehearsed disappears, leaving him with jumbled thoughts. Sally takes Little Jimmy and places him on her left hip holding him with one arm. She points at Jimmy with a scolding finger.

"I know you're going to the Crazy Horse and that's okay," she says. "But I worry. Sometimes when you drink you get really stupid. And I don't want my smart husband to get stupid drunk or be hanging out with Big Butch tomorrow."

Sally readjusts Little Jimmy and stands a little taller than her normal five-foot-four. She waits. It is Jimmy's turn and Jimmy knows that this is the moment, the turning point, the ball is in his court and how is he going to hit it back?

He thinks for a moment and the perfect response rolls off his tongue.

"I'll be with George," he says. "He's picking me up. And George never stays long."

And he thinks to himself that he is brilliant, fucking brilliant.

Sally laughs.

"Good answer, Jimmy. Don't be late for supper, it's Little Jimmy's favorite," she says. "My homemade macaroni and cheese with stewed tomatoes and fried haddock."

Jimmy seals the compromise by kissing Sally, expressing peace and harmony, and adds a kiss for Little Jimmy. His family turns and steps into the rest of the afternoon. Jimmy returns to work. The afternoon passes.

That evening, after Sally's delicious homemade macaroni and cheese and her light and flaky haddock, they sit at the kitchen table having coffee. She serves freshly-baked strawberry rhubarb pie with a glob of vanilla ice cream. Jimmy asks if she plans to bake something for George's birthday. Sally flashes a prideful smile.

"Of course. I was thinking of making another strawberry rhubarb pie. I still have some fresh rhubarb and I'll be going to the farmer's market with my mom and sister, so, I can get more strawberries."

"Oh, he'll love it," Jimmy says while chewing, "because this pie is more than delicious. It's scrumptious."

Sally is known for her pies. She comes from Pennsylvania Dutch stock. Her maiden name was Greenawalt and her mother was a Laudenslager. Sally's grandmother's recipes come straight from the Depression. Her mom stepped it up a little bit by using better-quality ingredients. Like Jimmy's place is in the garage with his Uncle Jack, Sally's is at home in the kitchen.

In the kitchen, her movements are of precision and grace— a cooking dance choreographed with pots and pans, skillets and baking sheets, flashing knives, stirring spoons, and rolling pins that squeeze the dough to the perfect thickness. Whoever comes to visit when Sally is cooking sits at the kitchen table and watches with amazement as she creates delicious and enjoyable foods from salad with hot bacon dressing to a crisp pig's stomach and homemade pearl tapioca pudding. Sally is happiest in her domain… the kitchen.

After a family walk around the block, Jimmy starts to get Little Jimmy ready for his bath. They start by getting the water to the right temperature and adding bubbles. Then, off with the clothing as Jimmy pretends to be astonished by how dirty Little Jimmy is. Next the toys, are thrown into the tub with a splash, the soap, washcloth, and finally Little Jimmy.

Jimmy lathers the washcloth and washes Little Jimmy, all the while Jimmy's singing:

"Neck bone connected to the shoulder bone, and shoulder bone connected to the arm bone, arm bone connected to that hand bone, them bones, them bones, them bones."

Little Jimmy giggles and tries to sing-along. When they get to the backbone connected to the heinie bone, little Jimmy releases a hearty two-year-old going-on-three laugh, the kind that throws his head back and Little Jimmy lets out a sound that indicates nothing else in the world matters but the enjoyment of the bone song and a heinie tickle.

Jimmy reaches for his son's toes to wash them.

"This Little Piggy," Jimmy says with a jiggle of the boy's big toe.

"Went to the playground," Little Jimmy responds jubilantly.

"And this little piggy," Jimmy continues across his son's foot. Little Jimmy giggles.

"Had macaroni and cheese," he decides.

"This little piggy?"

"Had to take a nap," Little Jimmy says.

"And this little piggy?"

"Ate ice cream cone!"

Jimmy wiggles the littlest toe.

"But this little piggy, this teeny-weeny, eany-beanie piggy," he says very earnestly, "this itsy-bitsy pinky piggy… this tiny, whiny, little bitty piggy went wee, wee, wee, wee, wee all the way home."

Little Jimmy giggles, laughs, and splashes. Jimmy tickles him under the chin.

"No, Daddy," Little Jimmy says. "No, Daddy. No, Daddy."

He holds up his plastic toy frog.

"'Joy to the world, all the boys and girls…'" Jimmy sings.

"Daddy, Daddy, Jeremiah Bullfrog broken his leg," Little Jimmy interrupts. "Look, Daddy, his leg is broken."

Sure enough, part of the frog's left rear leg is missing.

"Is he dead, Daddy?" the boy asks.

"No. No, he's not dead, he just broke his leg," Jimmy says. "Let's see if he can still swim. We'll just wind him up, put him in the water and let him go."

The frog doesn't swim in a straight line.

"Look, he's a circle swimmer now. He likes to swim in circles," Jimmy says. "Okay, time to dry off, hop out of the tub."

Little Jimmy stands on the bathroom rug, still trying to sing "Joy to the World."

Jimmy dries off the wet toddler, picks him up, grabs his pajamas, and down the stairs they go.

"Mommy, Little Jimmy's ready for a bedtime story," Jimmy says. "We're putting on his PJs."

Sally walks into the kitchen.

"Wow," she says to Little Jimmy. "Look how clean you are."

She leans down and gives Little Jimmy a kiss.

"Oh boy, you smell good, too."

Sally sits, straightens Little Jimmy's pajama top, and asks Jimmy when George is coming for him.

"Right about now," says Jimmy. "I'm going to wait for him on the porch."

Sally lifts Little Jimmy.

"We'll go upstairs and read a bedtime story," she says. "Give Daddy a kiss goodnight because he is going away with George."

Jimmy kisses Sally, then Little Jimmy, and walks toward the front door.

"Don't be too late and be careful," Sally calls after him. "Love you."

Jimmy opens the door. He turns back.

"Love you, too," he says to Sally, and then he gazes at Little Jimmy. "Goodnight, tadpole."

Jimmy steps out, closing the door behind him.

Sally stands at the kitchen doorway, holding Little Jimmy on her hip and staring at the closed door.

"God please keep him safe," she says, "and don't let him do anything stupid."

Sally kisses Little Jimmy on the cheek and rubs her belly.

Last year, in the summer of '73, Jimmy totaled his 1971 Chevelle, the first brand-new car he ever bought. He went through a stop sign and another car hit him in the left quarter panel, spinning the car around and taking out a telephone pole. Jimmy broke his arm and suffered a concussion. When Sally got to the hospital, Jimmy was handcuffed to the stretcher and yelling obscenities. She was ashamed, embarrassed, and brokenhearted.

Jimmy got arrested for driving under the influence, leaving him with a stiff fine and no license for a year. He was always an unpredictable drunk. Most of the time, he was fun and in good humor, but you never knew when the nasty miserable drunk would emerge. Sally knew this before they got married, but she had a vision, or a dream, that she could change him, and as she put it…"To see the real Jimmy, not the sick and confused one."

She thought, or you might say she hoped, that the car accident and being arrested would have changed him, or at least slowed him down. But it didn't. Jimmy's not an everyday drunk, but he is more than a once-a-week drunk.

Jimmy stands on the edge of the porch and lights a cigarette. He sighs as he blows out the match. Once more, thoughts of Big Butch come into his head. He looks up at the night sky and sees all the millions of stars.

"Big Butch, are you up there? I think you are," Jimmy says to the sky. "So, do you have any of them angel powers yet? Well, if you do, do you think you can help me…not to be such an asshole tonight?"

Jimmy hears the distinct sound of George's '68 Dodge Charger as it turns the corner. He steps off the porch. As he gets to the curb, a shiny, red Dodge pulls up slowly with a haunting low rumble. Jimmy gets in. He shakes George's hand.

"The old Charger looks good. How is she running, good?" he asks.

"Yeah," said George. "If you take some time and keep up with her, she'll run forever."

"I remember when you first got her," Jimmy says. "We were over at Big Butch's hanging out when you pulled up with Jeannie. You had the biggest shit-eating grin on your face. We were all like, 'Holy shit a Dodge!' We never even knew you liked Dodge. At least I never heard you speak of wanting one. It was wild."

"Yeah, I sure as hell didn't plan on buying it. You know, just got out of the Army and we walked into the car dealer for shits and giggles and the next thing you know, I'm driving a brand-new shiny, red, super stock, Dodge. What a trip!" George says, "Hey, I got half a joint here. You want to smoke a little bit?"

"Sure, fire it up," says Jimmy.

George reaches into the ashtray and pulls out the half a joint and hands it to Jimmy. Then, George gives him a smooth yellow porcelain disk, a little bit bigger than a half dollar and about a quarter of an inch thick.

"What the hell is this?" Jimmy asks.

"Smoking stone," says George.

"What the hell is a smoking stone?"

"See the holes on the edge?" George instructs. "You stick the joint in one of the holes and on the other end is where you suck the smoke through. It acts like a roach clip, but it's supposed to cool the smoke."

"You are shitting me. Cools the smoke? Who told you that?"

"Psychedelic Willy," George says with a laugh.

"Only Willy would have something like this."

"No. Try it, it works pretty nice."

Jimmy follows the instructions and sticks the joint in the end of the smoking stone and lights it. As he exhales, he coughs out, "Not bad and when did you see Willy?"

"The other day, when I bought this pot and he gave me this smoking stone."

"I want to get a hold of him. His grandfather has a '63 Falcon station wagon for sale and Willy said it's pretty nice," Jimmy says. "I want to get it for Sally, but it's supposed to be a surprise so don't say anything to Jeannie. You know Sally and Jeannie can't keep a secret."

Jimmy takes another hit.

"The last time I saw Willy," Jimmy says, "he comes to the back of the house. It's lunchtime and there's a knock on the door. So, I open it and it's Willy standing there with his long hair, red bandanna, beard, his two front teeth missing, and his round hippie glasses are sliding down his nose. He's wearing a tie-dye T-shirt and cutoff jeans. It was one of them hot days we had in April. You know he's looking like Willy should…"

"Sounds like Willy," George interjects.

"He pulls out this long strip of rolling paper. It's like a roll of stamps. He's standing there with this long rolling paper in front of him and he says in his funny nasal voice, 'Hey, you want to roll a joint?' I know Sally's walking up behind me, so I'm motioning for him to put away the rolling papers and he does."

"Oh, man," George says.

"He comes into the kitchen and says hi to Sally and you know she always gets a little freaky when Psychedelic Willy's around. But to my surprise, Sally says, 'We're just going to have lunch, it's grilled cheese and tomato soup.' Just that quick, without missing a beat, Willy says, 'Far out man, my favorite.' And he sits down, right next to Little Jimmy, and he says, 'Hey little dude, what's happening?' Little Jimmy shows him the Cheerios on his highchair tray and Willy says, 'Far out, they're one of my favorites, too.' So, Willy stays for lunch."

George asks, "Sal is ok with all this?"

Jimmy snickers. "Yeah, to my surprise I think things are going fine. Little Jimmy adores him and Willy enjoys talking with Little Jimmy. So, we're done with lunch, and Sally's cleaning off the table, she notices that Willy's balls are peeking out of his cutoffs."

George laughs. "Sally sees his balls sticking out of his cutoffs? Freakin' classic Willy."

"So, Sally gives me the high sign and the hairy eyeball," Jimmy continues. "I get Willy out of the kitchen and go out on the back porch with Willy and have a beer. When he leaves Sally says, 'What's wrong with him? He doesn't wear underwear! And his leg is always bouncing up and down. Sometimes he'll answer a question or make a comment about something that was in the conversation five minutes ago. He is weird. What's with the no underwear? I know he's your high school friend, but he is weird.'"

Through laughter, George says, "Yeah, Jeannie's the same way around Willy. Willy is weird. You can't help but love him. I wonder if he's going to Big Butch's viewing."

"Wonder if he even knows about it," Jimmy says.

"He just might be there. He always has a way of showing up when you least expect him."

"Hey, did you talk with Big Butch's parents?"

"No. But I think Jeannie sent them a card."

"Man, I don't know what to say…" Jimmy says. "'Sorry your kid is dead.'"

"I know what you mean."

"We seen guys die in 'Nam. But this is hitting me harder. It's different, old Stanley called it a chaos of emotion."

"Yeah, it's the same for me," George says.

George pulls the Charger into the parking lot. They get out of the car and into the warm night air, the smell of cheesesteaks and french fries reaches through the exhaust fan and streams across the parking lot. They're silent as they walk toward the flashing neon sign of a big red horse. Jimmy has a hurry in his step and George follows. Jimmy pulls the door open and a smile comes to his face as they walk in. The bar sounds of chattering voices, glasses clinking, and Linda Ronstadt singing "Silver Threads and Golden Needles" makes Jimmy's smile even grow bigger.

Pop, an older gray-haired man with a crew cut and a long goatee, sits on a barstool at the door and cards the people. He smiles when he greets Jimmy with a hello. Jimmy shakes his hand and pats his shoulder and asks how he's doing.

"Okay. No sense in complaining," Pop replies. "Nobody's really going to listen to you anyways."

Jimmy tells him "catch you later," which means that he'll send him a beer. George nods to Pop and follows Jimmy down the crowded aisle between the bar and the booths. As they make their way to the end of the bar, Jimmy stops several times to say hello or to make a humorous comment to people with drinks and cigarettes in hand. Jimmy waves to the bartender and points to the two empty stools near the end of the bar. The bartender nods his acknowledgment. When Jimmy and George get to the barstools, there's two beers waiting.

In one motion, Jimmy saddles up on the barstool and puts money on the bar. George stands at the barstool and takes his wallet out, fumbling with the bills. He sets his money on the bar before he sits on the stool.

"What's up, Sticks?" Jimmy says to the bartender. "Take the beers out of this and give Pop one on me."

"Not much happening, Jimmy. Just another crazy night at the Crazy Horse."

Sticks hustles away and Jimmy turns to George and says, "I love that guy. He's a great bartender."

Sticks got his name from a short tour with the Checkmates as a drummer in the early Sixties which gave him local fame. But most people think he got the name for playing the bottles and glasses behind the bar with drumsticks. His thick dirty blonde hair and beard give him a Kris Kristofferson look. He always wears a black leather vest with a pack of Camels in one pocket and a lighter in the other. He may give the appearance of being laid-back, but he takes the bar business very seriously. He's in his mid-thirties, so he's a bit older than the crowd at the Crazy Horse and has an uncanny wisdom that he shares freely. As Jimmy puts it, he's a trusted friend and cheaper than a head shrinker. He also has the best damn jukebox in town.

As Jimmy sips his beer, a relaxed feeling comes to him. It is like the relief most people get when they enter their house after a long trip. That safe feeling of being home comes to Jimmy when he sits on a barstool. Then you add his best friend George, the only man that he really trusts, and you just might get a glimpse of the real Jimmy. Jimmy puts his elbow on the bar and looks at George.

"Did you hear from Cheesy?" Jimmy asks. "I wonder if he knows about Big Butch."

"I talked to him about two weeks ago. He got promoted to a management position and he's doing something with computers," George answers. "As he puts it, he's no longer in the halls chasing crooks and hookers out of the hotel. He said he is coming home in August like he always does."

"I still can't get over Cheesy becoming a hotel dick in D.C."

"And a Republican," George quickly adds. "I wonder what he thinks about this whole Nixon thing with Watergate."

"Now they're talking about impeaching him," Jimmy says. "Life is a fucking circus sometimes."

"I think it doesn't much matter who's in office," George says. "Big business runs the fuckin' country anyway."

Sticks comes over and asks if they're ready for another beer. George says yes and taps his money on the bar. Sticks quickly returns with two cold beers. Jimmy asks him if he heard about Big Butch.

"No."

Jimmy tells him the story.

Sticks reacts with "Holy shit only twenty-seven years old. That's fucked up."

"This is affecting me more than I thought it would," Jimmy says. "I've experienced death before. But this has really shaken me up. You know what I mean?"

Sticks looks at Jimmy. "Maybe it's some shit that's stirring up from 'Nam."

"No, it's different," Jimmy says. "It's more like a little part of me is gone."

Sticks pours out three shots of tequila, putting slices of lemon and a salt shaker on the bar.

"To Big Butch," Sticks says.

All three men lick the salt, down the shots, and suck the lemons. Sticks puts his hands on the edge of the bar and leans forward a little.

"It's the first," he says dramatically. "Big Butch is the first of your childhood friends to die. It makes you look, really look, at your immortality. Anything that is the first is special. First kiss, first car, first time you got an award, the first time you hit a home run, first time you got suspended from school, first time you got high, the first time you got laid. Think about your kids. First step they took, first tooth, first time they shit on the potty. Firsts, there's something special about it. And Big Butch's death is going to touch you deep and surprise you when you least expect it."

Sticks lights up one of his Camels, throws quarters on the bar, and tells them to play the jukebox. He smiles and walks away. Jimmy and George look at each other.

"Guess he's right," Jimmy says.

The rest of the night is spent talking to old friends, playing the jukebox and singing along with the songs. Jimmy looks at the clock on the wall at just about 11 p.m.

"One more beer and one more song, then we'll hit the road," he tells George.

George looks at Jimmy in disbelief. Jimmy just hops off the bar-stool and puts a quarter in the jukebox. They drink their beer without speaking, and listen to the jukebox where John Prine sings "Sam Stone." And when he gets to the last time he sings "There's a hole in daddy's arm…," they know it is time to call it a night.

Not much is said on the ride home. Jimmy's thoughts conjure up images of their youth and visions of death. When they get to Jimmy's house, Jimmy thanks George for driving.

Then, Jimmy adds, "We'll see you on Friday for Big Butch's viewing… Oh, it's your birthday on Friday, too. I guess you won't feel like celebrating."

"No, I won't be celebrating much," George says. "Maybe some cake with Jeannie and the kids. Thanks again, I do appreciate it."

"No problem. It was a good night. See you on Friday."

George pulls away. Jimmy walks to the back door, puts his key in, and opens the door carefully. From the kitchen doorway, he can see the glow of the television and the illuminated silhouette of Sally curled up on the sofa. Jimmy closes the door. Sally becomes startled.

"Jimmy?" she calls out.

"Yeah, I'm home."

Sally gets up from the sofa and shuffles through the darkness of the dining room toward the kitchen. Jimmy turns on the light and can see Sally clearly now. There's a waddle to her walk with her belly stick-ing way out leading the way. She has on her pink flannel nightgown with images of ducks and her favorite brown rabbit slippers. Halfway through the dining room she speaks.

"I didn't expect you home this early," Sally says, with tiredness in her voice. "Everything okay?"

"Yeah, everything's okay."

Jimmy sits to take off his shoes. Sally enters the kitchen and stands by his side, stroking his deep brown hair. She tells him that she's glad he came home at a decent hour. When his shoes are off, Jimmy stands and puts his arms around Sally. She stands on her toes and they kiss.

"Do you want anything to eat?" she asks.

"No, honey. I just want to go to bed and hold you."

They kiss again, but this time it is longer.

"You go ahead upstairs," Sally says. "I'll turn off the TV."

Jimmy does. Sally comes into the bedroom asking if he had a good time at the Crazy Horse. Jimmy hangs his pants.

"Sure, I always have a good time with George," he says without turning around. "I like drinking there. Sticks is a good bartender and the jukebox is really great."

Sally is confused why Jimmy is home earlier than usual. But she knows she shouldn't just ask it out right. She knows she must set the stage for Jimmy's explanation, if there is any…so she waits.

They get into bed and as usual, after their good night kiss, they snuggle up to their spoon position. There is silence for three or four minutes.

"You know Sticks said something that was interesting tonight," Jimmy tells Sally. "He said the reason Big Butch's death is so… aww, what's the word I'm looking for… moving, important? Oh, I don't know. Meaningful? It's that he is the first friend, from all the guys I grew up with, to die."

"Yeah?" Sally says.

"I experienced death with my grandmother, my Uncle Bob and I even saw death firsthand in Vietnam, but this is different. Butch is the first real friend I grew up with to die. Then he said the first of anything is incredibly special, you know like the first kiss, the first time you hit a home run, a child's first tooth. Guess there's truth to it."

"So, what do you feel about Big Butch's death?" asks Sally.

"There's a part of me that's gone," Jimmy admits. "The part that can never have a conversation with Big Butch about things that we shared. From now on it will be one-sided."

"You have other friends to share things with," Sally says. "Not just Big Butch."

"But I'll never have the private one-on-one talks which happen only at special times," he says.

"What do you think about what Sticks said about the first time being important?"

"That is absolutely true," Jimmy says. "Look at the first time we kissed. I mean really kissed. That's when we fell in love, on our first romantic kiss."

Sally giggles.

"You don't even remember our first romantic kiss," she states.

"Yes, I do," Jimmy insists.

"When?"

"Was on the hayride when we were seniors. You got cold and snuggled up to me and we started to kiss. And that was it, you were in my power."

Sally quickly turns to face Jimmy.

"You are so full of shit," she says.

They laugh, embrace and kiss.

Thursday, May 23, 1974

Jimmy opens his eyes and gazes at the clock on the dresser with a morning squint.

"Oh, shit!" Jimmy shouts. "Sally, I don't want to be late today."

Jimmy jumps out of bed. He grabs the pants hanging on the hook behind the bedroom door and starts to get dressed. Sally lumbers from the bed.

"You have time, slow down," she says.

"I want to be there when Jack gets there."

"Why?"

"Because he knows I went out last night and he expects me to be hung over."

"Don't be silly," Sally says. "He can tell if you're hungover or not."

"I guess he can," Jimmy says. He turns to her and pauses. "I still want to be there. First."

Sally hurries downstairs. Sally shakes her head in disapproval as Jimmy, in his stocking feet, slides across the kitchen floor to the chair where he sits to put on his work boots. Sally looks at him sternly.

"You're going to have a cup of coffee and some toast," she says. "It's only going to take a minute."

Jimmy sighs. They hear the bump-thump, bump-thump, bump-thump of Little Jimmy on the stairs. Jimmy goes to the bottom. Sally heads into the kitchen and puts bread in the toaster.

"Come on, tadpole," Jimmy tells his son.

He scoops the boy into his arms and carries him into the kitchen. With a smile, Little Jimmy exclaims that it's breakfast time and announces that he wants Cheerios with blueberries.

Jimmy's anxiousness dissolves with the love of Little Jimmy.

"Cheerios with blueberries! They are the bests of the best!" Jimmy says loudly.

Then, he whispers into Little Jimmy's ear that Cheerios and blueberries always taste much better if you ask for them politely.

"If you ask mommy please, it will taste much better."

Little Jimmy giggles.

"Mommy, please Cheerios and blueberries."

Sally smiles.

"Okay," she says.

She gets the blueberries from the refrigerator. Everybody settles around the table. They eat Cheerios and blueberries, and toast, and coffee for the grown-ups.

Sally has the urge to ask Jimmy, why is it so important for him to impress Jack this morning? Why is this morning any different from any other morning? She remains silent and lets her questions fade. But then tries to engage him in conversation.

"Don't forget," Sally says. "Little Jimmy and I are going to visit my mom and go to the farmer's market today. So, you're on your own for lunch."

Jimmy nods and thanks Sally for breakfast. He kisses her and Little Jimmy goodbye and out the door he goes.

When Jimmy gets to the garage, Jack is sitting on a stool sipping a cup of coffee.

"Good morning, Jimmy," Jack says.

"Good morning," says Jimmy.

"I was thinking that we get all the mechanical work done first and road test her before we do any more bodywork. That way we'll get the greasy stuff done and we won't have to mess with her after she's painted and pretty," Jack says. "So, do you think you can do the brakes? The new shoes and whatnot are over there in that box. I don't think they're much different than any other brakes, so I think we'll be okay."

"Sure, sounds like a plan to me," Jimmy says.

Without another word, they get to work. Besides the radio in the background with Early Whirly in the Morning on WAEB, the sounds of working men is all you hear. But in Jimmy's head, he questioned why Jack didn't ask him about last night. He didn't even ask if he had a good time with George. There is an insistent eagerness to tell Jack that he didn't get wasted last night. But he holds his tongue, focusing on work. It was common for long periods without conversation while they were working, but today their silence encourages the voices that battle within Jimmy's brain.

Every so often he chants an inner mantra, "I'm not a fuck-up, I'm not a drunk."

When the sports report with Ernie Stigler comes on the radio, their silence breaks. Pappy Jack steps into the garage.

"What's happening here at Jack's Restoration?" Pappy asks.

Jimmy gives a push and rolls back on his work stool. Relief from his nagging thoughts and self-induced tension subsides when he hears Pappy Jack. Jimmy walks over to his grandfather and gives him a hug. He feels secure. Pappy Jack has a current of hopeful energy. Jimmy always feels safe and loved by Pappy Jack.

When Jimmy was five or six, his mother, Eleanor, who went by Ellie, and his father, Joe "Skeeter" Washburn, got divorced. Skeeter moved to California and eventually got married and started a new family. So, Jimmy didn't spend much time with his father, and Pappy Jack stepped in and played the father role.

In the 1950s, it was hard for a single mother, and the stigma of divorcée. Eleanor worked hard at the tax office for the city of Bethlehem and did hairdressing on the side for friends and neighbors. She did the best she could with Jimmy, he was always on the wild side.

Pappy Jack was there to help things along. Ellie asked Jack to give fourteen-year-old Jimmy a job, so she knew where he was and that he was out of trouble. That summer, Jimmy started to work in the garage with his Uncle Jack.

Pappy Jack stands with his arms folded. He speaks loud enough so that Jack can hear him on the other side of the Buick.

"Well, what have we here?" Pappy remarks.

"Take a guess," the younger Jack says. "Do you still know your stuff?"

"Well, it's a Buick, that's easy enough," Pappy says. "Looks like it's a higher-priced Buick by the dual fender wells and all the chrome. I'll guess it's a Buick Roadmaster. '36, maybe '37… no, a '38."

"Pretty good, Dad," Uncle Jack says. "It's a '38 Buick Roadmaster model 81 touring sedan, with the Dynaflash straight eight, 141 horsepower."

"This is a good one," Pappy says. "Who owns her?"

"That guy from up in Northampton, he had that '28 blue Essex we did."

"Oh, Pete Kemmerer," Pappy says.

"Yeah, that's the guy," Jack confirms.

"It's good to see that he's still fooling around with cars. I came to take you two fellas to lunch. Can you break away? We'll go to Lucy's, haven't been there for a while."

"Sounds good to me," said Jimmy. "What do you say, Jack?"

"Okay, but I'd like to road-test her first," he says.

Uncle Jack and Pappy Jack finish bleeding the brakes while Jimmy puts on a license plate and hooks up the brake lights. Like that, she was ready to roll. Pappy Jack pulls her out of the garage slow and tests the brakes. Jack and Jimmy pile in and down the alley they roll. Pappy Jack drives around the block two times and then he starts up the hill to Main Street. Jack looks at Pappy Jack.

"Where in the hell are we going?" Uncle Jack asks.

"Lunch, this will be fun," Pappy replies.

When they turn the corner onto Main Street, they see Stanley going into Bucky's Place. Jimmy tells Pappy Jack to honk the horn. Stanley turns to look. They yell and wave. Stanley politely bows to them as they drive past.

Pappy Jack laughs.

"Same old Stanley. I know him since the thirties when he bartended on Hamilton Street. Paydays we would stop in to cash our checks and have free lunch. At that time, barrooms cashed payroll checks, especially on Friday or Saturday. They would put a spread out of cold meat and cheese, pickled eggs, bread, and butter," Pappy Jack says, lost in his memories. "The bar would be crowded with Mack workers. It was the Depression and to get a few days or a week of work was grand… everybody was in a hurry but Stanley…"

Jimmy listens carefully. It doesn't matter how many times he hears the stories.

"…Stanley always took his time, never got flustered. If somebody started to get on his nerves, Stanley would sing," Pappy continues. "Sometimes Stanley would sing a silly song about 'weight broke the wagon' and 'St. Peter's always there.' Something about time goes at the same speed no matter if you walk or run. He was a good singer. He sang in a barbershop quartet, with Buckets O' Donald, Preacher Rome, and Duie Page. They called themselves 'The Sometimes Gentlemen' because sometimes they would sing naughty and bawdy songs. Funny, but a little raunchy."

They pull into the parking lot at Lucy's Light Lunch. Pappy Jack confirms that the Buick runs well. When they walk into Lucy's, they find Frosty Wallace and Clarence Peters sitting at the counter. Frosty is short and pudgy. He wears tan Dickie work pants, a reddish flannel plaid shirt, an old light green Dickie work jacket, and a faded Phillies baseball cap to hides his baldness. Clarence is tall, thin, and balding. He has on bib overalls, and an old blue pin-striped dress shirt with a frayed collar. On the stool next to him rests a light denim barn coat and an old, soft felt fedora hat. You could say they look like the Pennsylvania Dutch version of a Bert and Harry Piels beer commercial. Clarence speaks in a Pennsylvania Dutchified accent.

"Why just look at this, two Jacks and a Jimmy," he says. "That's one hell of a poker hand. Why by Jesus I should say, we're in for some trouble now."

Pappy Jack, Jack and Jimmy go to Frosty and Clarence, greeting them with handshakes and "how's it going," "good to see you."

"Still kicking," Frosty says. "No sense in complaining, nobody really gives a goddamn anyway."

"We're a hell of a lot better than President Nixon," says Clarence. "Why that Watergate business! It's like Mother Goose sending her children out to steal dirty underwear and they all get caught with their pants down…aye yai yai! I just can't believe it."

"You got to remember he's not a crook," Pappy Jack replies.

The room erupts in laughter. As it subsides, Jack picks a table. If Frosty or Clarence turn their heads to the left, they can all see each other. Lucy hands out the menus and rattles off the lunch specials.

"We have hot turkey sandwiches, chicken pot pie, and shepherd's pie," she announces.

With business matters aside, she asks how everybody is doing and if the families are well.

Lucy and her husband, Luther, have run Lucy's Light Lunch since 1958. Originally their home, they turned the downstairs into a luncheonette and moved themselves upstairs. Lucy is sixty, medium height and build, with gray curly hair. She wears a house dress with a full flower print apron and brownline glasses, blue on the top and clear on the bottom. She still moves with the energy of a twenty-five-year-old. Luther sits at the cash register looking like William Bendix in The Life of Riley, reads the newspaper, and smokes Chesterfield cigarettes. He's two years older and much more reserved than outgoing Lucy. Some people take him as being rude or antisocial.

"Who made the chicken pot pie?" Pappy Jack asks.

Lucy laughs.

"Why me!" she answers. "Who else would make it?"

"I just want to make sure," Pappy says in a serious voice, "that your grumpy husband had nothing to do with it."

Again, Lucy laughs.

"He has nothing to do with anything," she says. "All he can do is sit at that register and collect the money."

"I hope he's honest," Pappy says.

"So do I," says Lucy.

Pappy Jack and Jimmy ordered the chicken pot pie and Uncle Jack gets a hot turkey sandwich. Clarence swings around on his stool away from the counter.

"Say, did you hear about Rollie Diefenderfer?"

And in unison, the boys reply, "No."

Frosty swings around. "Why sure, he was on the Dopey Duncan radio show."

"Well, you see, they was playing a game like Name That Tune," Clarence continues. "Dopey Duncan would sing part of a song then stop. And you have to say the next word and spell it."

"They start off with an easy one, Old McDonald," Frosty says.

Without missing a beat, Clarence carries on. "Dopey sings, 'Old McDonald had a...'"

Very seriously, Frosty leans forward. "The first lady that buzzed in says 'Pig, P. I. G.'"

Clarence now hits Frosty on the arm and gives him a dirty look.

"Well, Dopey says, 'you spelled it right but it's the wrong word,'" Clarence tells.

Clarence gives Frosty another dirty look.

"Well he says 'we'll try it again,'" Clarence says. "And again, Dopey sings, 'Old McDonald had a...' The next fellow buzzes in and says, 'Dog, D.O. G.' Well, he says, 'you spelled it right but it's the wrong word. We'll try her one more time,' and Dopey sings, 'Old McDonald had a...' And now Rollie Defenderfer buzzes in and says—"

At the same time, Frosty and Clarence yell: "'Why that's an easy one now. It's farm... E. I. E. I. O.'"

Everybody laughs. Even Lucy's grumpy husband, Luther, laughs. Frosty and Clarence finish their pie and coffee, say goodbye to everybody, and out the back door they go. Pappy Jack leans to Jimmy, close to his ear.

"Those hoof-tees been telling that joke since the 1940s," he whispers.

Lucy brings the order and sets it down in front of them.

"Them two come in here every day and they always have a story to tell," she says. "I don't always understand what they're talking about but they're entertaining, that's for sure."

"They been best friends since they were kids," says Pappy Jack. "They only lived a block away from each other and they still only live a block away from each other. Clarence gave Frosty his nickname Frosty, because his hair was so white when he was a kid. They married sisters, Rose and Iris. Their wives died but they're still best friends."

Jimmy eats his potpie and thinks of his best friend, George. They didn't marry sisters, but he wonders what they will be like when they're old men like Frosty and Clarence. Thoughts of Big Butch seep into his feelings. He can envision Big Butch, standing, laughing, with a beer in his hand. He can hear his voice.

Jimmy has the urge to say aloud, "I wish you wouldn't have died."

But Jimmy turns to Pappy Jack and asks if he remembers his friend Big Butch. Jimmy tells him the story of the death of Big Butch, that he was only twenty-seven years old, and in a heartbeat that he was gone. Pappy Jack looks Jimmy in the eyes.

"That's sad. It's really sad," Pappy says. "You must be hurting and confused. I don't want to sound like a cliché or bullshit, but you might be surprised what can come from this."

"What do you mean?" Jimmy asks.

"Well, the first thing that comes to mind is when your grandmother and I were only married a short time, my father-in-law, your grandmother's father, Bill, passed away. He was sick for a while, so we were prepared for his death. But within a week my father, your great-grandfather Johnathan, suddenly died from a heart attack," Pappy tells him. "But out of these two tragedies came a blessing. Although my mother, Betty, and Dorothy, your grandmother's mother, didn't really know each other, they became best friends. They helped each other get over their grief and learn to live life without their husbands. This made them much stronger women."

"But don't you think it would have been better if their husbands would have lived?" Jimmy asks.

"I don't know for sure. My guess would be yes, it would be better if they wouldn't have died. But that's not what happened, they did die," Pappy answers. "I do know, from their death, two women became much stronger women and they had a happy life despite their sadness. Jimmy, I don't want to take away your grief, and I don't want to take away the memory of your good friend. I do feel for you. I'm just saying don't be surprised if something good just might come out of this."

Jimmy nods and eats his chicken pot pie. He doesn't say much at lunch or for the rest of the day. At the garage, he does his work quietly and listens to the radio. He thinks about friendship. Memories of adolescent boys sharing their secrets. Jimmy couldn't put it into words, but he now understands that vulnerability is part of friendship, as is trust and loyalty. Jimmy realizes that sometimes, he is not always the good friend that he thought he was. He questions himself, asking, is this part of the grief that I feel?

Today, Jimmy doesn't go up the hill to Bucky's and have a beer with Stanley. He is cut off from his daily routine by the emotions that spiral within his mind. Today, he intuitively knows that the best place for him is at home. And when he walks into the house, he scoops Little Jimmy off the floor, and hugs and kisses him.

"You are the bestest of the best," says Jimmy.

He hugs and kisses him until Little Jimmy giggles and squirms.

"Stop, Daddy, stop."

Jimmy does stop and then goes to Sally. He holds her in his arms, kisses her, and tells her that she's the best wife he ever had. Sally laughs. Jimmy holds her tighter.

"It's true, it's true, it's true I tell you," he shouts.

Sally laughs more.

"Jimmy, don't hold me this tight," she protests, "or the baby might pop out."

Jimmy releases Sally. She takes a half a step back. Cocking her head slightly to the side, looking from the corners of her eyes, she gives a sneering smile that says: "I know something is going on with you, but I'm not asking."

Jimmy responds to her unspoken statement. "What?"

Sally quickly changes to a smile of gratitude.

"I'm glad you're home."

After supper, Jimmy plays with Little Jimmy in the yard. They play with trucks, and then a big red ball. They end with Jimmy pulling Little Jimmy in a wagon. They pretend to stop at ice cream stands, toy stores, and Uncle Jack's garage. When they come in the house, Sally says that it's time for a bath. Jimmy hustles Little Jimmy upstairs. Their imagination and creativity continue as they play and splash in the tub, almost neglecting to scrub.

When Little Jimmy is finally put to bed, it's Sally and Jimmy's time for themselves. They plop in front of the TV, Sally with a soda and Jimmy with a beer, settling in to watch *Kung Fu* with David Carradine. Jimmy wouldn't say this is one of his favorite shows, but he does enjoy watching it. And Sally, though it's not her favorite either, will sit with Jimmy, as she said, glad to have him home.

After the show, Jimmy gets up and stretches.

"You know, Sal, it is true, the part where Grasshopper was being instructed to shoot the bow and arrow. His instructor told him to visualize the arrow leaving the bow, sailing through the air, and hitting the bull's-eye. That the arrow was part of him. It's like seeing it hit the bull's-eye before it happens," he tells her. "You know when I paint, the spray gun becomes part of me, kind of an extension of my hand. And I do see the paint mist hit the surface of the car and flow out before it actually happens. There is a magic when I paint, I'm focused and there's nothing else to distract me. It's intense, but I'm at peace at the same time."

Jimmy sits, folding his arms like a pouting child.

"Why can't I have more moments like that in other parts of my life?" he asks.

"But you do, Jimmy," she says. "When you play with Little Jimmy, you're right there with him. And we have our moments."

Jimmy unfolds his arms and moves closer to Sally. He leans forward as if to kiss her.

"We could have one of those moments right now," Jimmy says.

Sally rolls her eyes and gives that little smile, the sneer where the left corner of her mouth curls up.

This is the smile that says, "listen up, stupid."

"It's not always about sex, Jimmy," she explains. "We have some really good times. We laugh a lot and enjoy each other. Our family has a special love."

Jimmy puts his head on Sally's lap, looking up at her with his ear against her belly as if to listen to the baby.

"I think this baby is going to be a real free spirit and a talker," says Jimmy.

"Why do you say that?" Sally asks.

"This one's different than Little Jimmy," he says. "She moves around a lot more than Little Jimmy did. Like she has someplace to go and something to say."

"'She'?" Sally says almost immediately, almost interrupting him. "What makes you say 'she'? You never referred to the baby as 'she' before."

Jimmy pauses. He looks at Sally thoughtfully. He shrugs his shoulders and raises his eyebrows.

"I just have the feeling that it's going to be a girl," he says. "Hey, let's do the cork and needle thing. Where is your sewing box? There's a wine cork on the kitchen shelf."

"My sewing box is in the dining room, in the bottom of the dry sink. Why are you so wound up now?"

Jimmy returns with the cork, needle, and thread.

"Come on, lie flat on the floor and I'll hold it over your belly," he tells her.

With a groan, Sally gets on the floor. She lies flat with her arms at her side. Jimmy places the needle in the middle of the cork's larger end and stretches the white thread. He straddles Sally's belly.

"That's not how you do it, stand to the side," she says. "Do it the right way."

"What's the right way?" asks Jimmy.

"The Pennsylvania Dutch way. Stand at my side," directs Sally.

Jimmy stands with his feet together on her right side, above her hip, in line with her belly. He extends his right arm, bent at a right angle at the elbow and pinching the thread with his thumb and index finger, holding it directly over Sally's belly. The weight of the cork acts like a plum-bob and pulls the thread tight and straight down.

"I hold it over your belly about a foot and a half in the air," Jimmy says very seriously. "They say if it swings in a circle, it's a girl, and if it moves back-and-forth, it's a boy. Okay, here we go."

Jimmy straightens the thread and holds it firmly over Sally's belly. Nobody says a word and they're not breathing. And the quiet! It's so quiet that it seems mysteriously spiritual.

The cork starts to move. First with a quiver and then with the motion of a small circle, slow and steady. The rotation broadens. It is easy to see that it's moving in a circular motion.

"You're doing that," Sally says with a scornful smile.

"No, I'm not. Honest. It's moving on its own. It's a girl."

"This is silly. Help me up."

Sally gets to her feet. Jimmy holds her and gives her a kiss. Jimmy looks at Sally.

"I really do think it's a girl," he says again.

"I have no idea," Sally says. "I try not to think about it. But whatever it is, I want it to be healthy. And to have a good life. Let's go to bed."

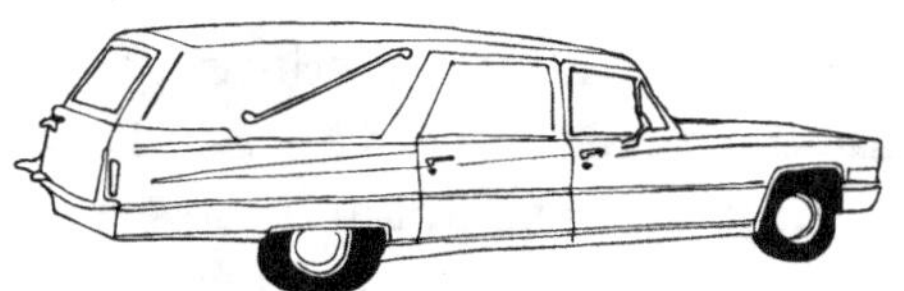

Friday, May 24, 1974

The next morning is a typical workday. Jimmy walks into the garage and sees Jack sitting on the stool by the workbench sipping a coffee. They exchange good mornings and Jack starts to explain the plan.

"Now that the rear fenders are done, you can finish sanding and spot-priming the rest of the body. I'll pull the hood, lights, and fenders. Then get everything ready in the engine compartment. You can help me when I need it. If we hustle, we can knock off today around 3 o'clock."

"Sounds good to me, Uncle Jack."

They both work hard and steady and not much is said until about 11 o'clock, when Jack asks Jimmy to give him a hand. He needs Jimmy to help remove the fenders. When the task is completed, Jimmy sits on a stool and lights a cigarette. Jack pours himself another cup of coffee.

"I suppose you're going to Big Butch's viewing tonight," Uncle Jack says.

"Yeah, Sal and I are going with George and Jeannie," Jimmy answers. "It's going to be pretty strange. Big Butch's parents must be freaking out."

"I suppose they are. But don't be too surprised if you find them smiling more than crying," Uncle Jack says. "You never know what you might find at an affair like that."

Jimmy sits for a moment.

"Jack, do you think there's a hereafter? Do you really think there's a heaven and a hell?"

"In a one-word answer, yes," Uncle Jack says. "I don't think it's so cut and dried as that. I do think how you live your life here on Earth is most definitely going to affect your fate in the hereafter."

"What do you mean?" Jimmy asks.

"It's like the basic law of nature. If you plant a seed in good soil, nurture it, water it, and make sure it gets plenty of sunshine, it will grow. If it grows good and healthy, it produces good and healthy seeds. When the plant dies, the seeds will move on and another plant will grow," Jack says. "Our life is the plant and the seeds are our soul. So, when we die our soul gets to grow again. Our life here is preparing our souls for the next adventure. Our life is the key that opens the door to our death."

Jimmy draws deep on his cigarette and blows the smoke down toward the ground.

"In other words, what I do or don't do in my life will affect my next life, if there is one. And that our bodies have to die so our souls can move on."

"Yeah, that's the way I look at it. But remember, the only thing that is for sure is a closed mind," Jack says. "When your mind is closed, you shut out opportunities and possibilities. If you have a closed mind about death, I would think you're going to be disappointed. But if you have an open mind about death, I would think that you will have a greater adventure. Being surprised is good."

Not much is said after that, but the pair work hard and conscientiously. Working right through lunch, they knock off around 2:30. They make sure that each step in their automotive undertaking is accurate so that the next step is even better, for they are master craftsmen. Jack locks up the garage.

"Hey, you want to go up to Bucky's and grab a beer?" Jimmy asks.

Jack turns with a pause, as if he might say yes. He looks at Jimmy.

"No," he says. "I got things I want to do in the garden and today's a good day to do it. Say hi to Stanley and don't stay too long. You got Big Butch's viewing tonight and you don't want to be going there half snookered up."

Jack goes down the two steps that lead to the yard. Jimmy stands and looks up the hill to Bucky's place. He wonders if Jack is always going to think of him as a kid. He has an anxious feeling that borders on desperation, wondering what Jack thinks of the future and if he is included. His self-doubt feeds the gnawing self-centered fear that Jimmy almost acknowledges but always pushes deeper within himself. If Jack weren't here, could he run the garage by himself, and is he really good at repairing cars? Jimmy starts his journey up the hill telling himself the fable that a few beers will mend his broken pride.

Jimmy walks into the bar room. Stanley greets him heartily.

"Hello, Jimmy!"

Jimmy walks to his usual perch. His fears are left outside like an angry dog waiting for its master. He sits and shakes Stanley's hand. Haasie sets a beer in front of Jimmy and asks if he needs a short one.

"No shots today," Jimmy replies. "I need to behave myself."

"Why is that?" Stanley says.

"Butch's viewing is tonight and as Uncle Jack puts it, I don't want to be going there half snookered up."

"I see," says Stanley, "Speaking of funerals, Duke Ellington passed away today. I just heard it on the radio. He was seventy-five, that's younger than me."

"I know him, my mom likes to listen to his music," Jimmy says. "That song 'A Train' was his hit."

"He wrote hundreds of songs," Stanley says. "'Sophisticated Lady,' 'Mood Indigo,' 'Creole Love Call' and so many more. Evie and I saw him in Allentown at the Colonial Theatre, in 1934, maybe '35, on Halloween night. I was working as a chauffeur at the time and my boss, Mr. Hornsby, gave me two tickets. So, I took Evie and we had a wonderful time. It was better than listening to him on the radio, that's for damn sure."

"I didn't know you're into jazz," Jimmy says.

"That may be called jazz, but it's just good music to me," Stanley says. "Say, what's on your mind, Jimmy?"

"What do you mean?"

"There's more to it than not having a shot because you're going to Big Butch's viewing."

"Yeah. You know I've been working for Uncle Jack twelve years since I was fourteen," Jimmy says. "Well, except for the two years I was in the Army. He treats me like a kid."

Stanley takes a sip of beer.

"Do you act like a kid?" he asks.

"No," Jimmy answers. "Well, maybe sometimes."

"If you want to be treated like an adult, you have to act like one," Stanley says." I worked for my father-in-law, Harry, for years in this very same bar. I started working for him part-time around 1927. I was about 35 years old. And at that time, I was quite a gadabout. I was a good bartender for him, but he never took me seriously. That was until I married Evie. Then, he hated me."

Jimmy laughs and asks why.

"You might know some of this," Stanley says, "when we got married, I was 40-years-old and Evie was only twenty-six and Harry thought of me as this good-time-Charlie kind of guy. He never trusted me. Evie and I worked for him until he sold the bar in 1954. Then we moved up here. It's Harry's house, not ours."

"Didn't you and Evie want to keep the bar?"

"No, I was sixty and Evie was damn near fifty. The bar business is hard work. It worked out well, with our little dry-cleaning business. The point I'm trying to make is that Harry had this opinion of me because I didn't take life as seriously as he did," Stanley says. "He was right, I am somewhat of a good-time-Charlie and I like being Stanley. I have fun most of the time and I didn't worry about things like he did. That was hard for him to understand. So, don't worry about your Uncle Jack. He will never do you wrong, he loves you. And if you do grow up a little bit, he will love you more."

Jimmy sits quietly through the next beer, and then he puts his coaster on top of his glass. No more beer for him. He motions for Haasie and tells him to get Stanley a beer out of his money. Stanley looks at Jimmy, a little confused. Jimmy hops off the barstool and pats Stanley on the back.

"Thanks, Stanley," Jimmy says. "I got to go home, have a little growing up to do."

Walking down the hill toward home, Jimmy feels a bit easier. The dogs of fear are no longer nipping at his heels. His thoughts turn to Sally and Little Jimmy. When he walks into the house, Sally and Little Jimmy are surprised to see him. Sally asks why he's home so early.

"Well, we got done a little early today," Jimmy replies in a nonchalant way.

Jimmy sits and unlaces his work boots. Sally stands in the middle of the kitchen floor with Little Jimmy on her hip. They both gaze at Jimmy with smiles of gratitude. Jimmy senses warm grateful energy coming from Sally and Little Jimmy. But it makes him uneasy.

"What is the plan for tonight?" Jimmy asks.

"Well," Sally says. "We have to meet George and Jeannie at seven o'clock, so my mom is coming over here at six."

Jimmy nods. "You want to make supper, or would you rather go out to eat?"

Sally laughs. "What do you think?"

Jimmy stands and smiles. He looks at Sally, realizing that he is not just looking at Sally with his eyes but he's seeing her with his heart.

"You look like a poster for motherhood."

Sally's eyes widen with surprise. "What do you mean?"

"Just look at you. There you are standing in the middle of the kitchen, holding a dirty-faced two-and-half-year-old on your hip," he says. "It's obvious that you're very pregnant with your belly sticking out all round and big, but you have this smile on your face. You're smiling and you're glowing like someone in a TV commercial. You know, like someone that just drank a Coke and now the world is wonderful."

Sally frowns. "No, no."

"It's the real thing," Jimmy says.

"It's the real thing," repeats Sally, "You were doing so good and I end up a freaking Coke commercial, jingle and all."

Jimmy walks to Sally and Little Jimmy and puts his arms around them. He kisses Sally on the forehead.

"No, Sally. You're not a Coke commercial," he says in a soft voice. "It came out all wrong. What I was trying to say was, just looking at you touched me. It went deep inside and I was so incredibly happy that you are my wife and mother of my children. I don't know how to say things like that. But I do know how I feel, and I love you."

They kiss. Little Jimmy squirms.

"Down. I want to get down."

Sally looks at Jimmy and her familiar sneer turns into a genuine smile.

"You said it just fine. It was perfect."

Later when waiting for Sally's mom, Gloria, to arrive, Sally darts quickly from room to room straightening and doing last minute things.

"Jimmy get your sport coat on," Sally directs him. "My mom is coming sooner than we said, since we're going out to eat. Oh, can you get the Go Dog Go book, please? Did you put George's pie in the car?"

Jimmy sits at the foot of the steps that lead to the second floor, draws on his cigarette, and then blows smoke rings into the air.

Sally marches by and then stops.

"What the hell are you doing?" she says in a low, agitated voice.

Jimmy strokes his mustache and lets smoke drift out of his nose.

"I'm resting and waiting," he says.

Sally stands with her hands on her hips.

"Resting and waiting for what?"

"For you to tell me what to do next."

Sally rolls her eyes.

"I did everything you told me to do," he says.

Sally gives him her "this is bullshit" expression, a frustrated sneer.

"You got the Go Dog Go book?" she asks.

"Yes. It's on the coffee table," Jimmy replies.

"You put the pie in the car?"

"Yes. Now, what is next?"

"Go over and sit on the sofa with Little Jimmy."

And with that, Sally dismisses Jimmy. Little Jimmy sits on the sofa smiling and full of excitement. Washed and with his hair combed, he wears his Grover pajamas, with Henny the monkey on his left and Buster Bear on his right. Books are piled on the coffee table, ready to be read. Gloria arrives shortly thereafter.

"Nana, you have cookies?" Little Jimmy asks.

Gloria laughs. Gloria stands a bit shorter than Sally and a few pounds heavier. Her hair is nicely styled in a blow-out that lets you know that she goes to the hairdresser every week.

"Yes, honey," she says. "I have cookies. AP cut out cookies in the shape of dogs, cats, cars, and trucks. We will eat cookies and read books."

Little Jimmy has eaten Gloria's APs many times. Those are her all-purpose cut-outs, the recipe she adapts for every occasion.

Little Jimmy jumps up and down on the sofa.

"YAY!"

Sally takes Little Jimmy's hand.

"Ok, ok. That is enough jumping," she says. "You sit nice with Nana, eat a cookie, and read books. Daddy and I are going out to dinner. We will be back after you're in bed. So you be a good boy."

Sally leans over and kisses Little Jimmy on the cheek. Jimmy does the same.

"Eat a car cookie for me," Jimmy whispers.

Little Jimmy smiles and nods yes. Sally and Jimmy slip out the door while Nana brings out the cookies.

Sally and Jimmy head to the Boulevard Inn restaurant. Jimmy picks out a corner table. It's more secluded, and he thinks it will be romantic. Annie, the waitress who has been there for years, hustles to them.

"I haven't seen you guys for a while," Annie says, "Oh, honey, look at you. You sure are pregnant, I feel like I need to get you a special chair. When are you due?"

Sally chuckles.

"Maybe next week," Sally says. "But I guess it could be any time."

"I wish you the best of luck," Annie says. "So, we have a nice cod fish broiled in butter with two vegetables; lasagna and you get a salad; and we have prime-rib with potato and veggies."

Without hesitation, Jimmy orders the lasagna and a Michelob. Sally asks for something light. Annie suggests a chef salad with shrimp instead of meat and squeezing some lemon wedges over it for dressing. Sally agrees. She asks for just water to drink. Jimmy pours his beer into the glass.

"We should have asked Jeannie and George to come to dinner," Sally says.

Jimmy sticks out his bottom lip a bit, wrinkles his nose, and shakes his head slightly.

"No. George needs to be with his family on his birthday. He said that they were going to have cake and ice cream with the kids before going to Big Butch's funeral."

"Oh, when did he say that?" Sally says with surprise in her voice. "Jeannie didn't mention it."

"When we went to the Crazy Horse," he says. "We talk about more than cars and shit. Sometimes we have meaningful conversations."

There is a pause. Jimmy and Sally laugh. Jimmy sips his beer.

"No really, we do talk about different stuff," he adds. "We both feel the same about Big Butch."

"What do you mean?"

"Well, we feel shocked and sad. But we both have this fucked up feeling that you can't describe," Jimmy says. "Loss is confusing. We just didn't misplace Big Butch. He's gone."

Without saying a word, Sally reaches over and takes Jimmy's hand. They sit in silence till Annie comes bustling over with their order.

"Ok, the gent gets the lasagna and the lady is a light salad with shrimp. Is there anything else I can get for you?" she asks.

"Yes, another Michelob," Jimmy says.

When Annie goes to get the beer, Sally leans over the table.

"Jimmy," she says in a low voice, "you didn't even finish this beer and you're ordering another one? Besides we are going to a funeral."

"I know you don't want me to be all snookered up," he says. "But I'm not driving, you are."

Sally stares at him with a look of disapproval, and her sneer says 'stop this shit.'

Jimmy wipes the beer foam from his mustache.

"You're right," he says. "I'm not going to drink anymore."

He changes the conversation to how good the food is. While they eat, the tension subsides and by the end of dinner, they're smiling and in love again. They continue to the funeral home. Sally pulls the car into a crowded parking lot.

"Wow, look at all the cars," Sally says.

"You know, Sal, Big Butch was loved by a lot of people."

"It sure looks that way. Look, there is Jeannie and George. I'll pull over there."

She pulls beside George and Jeannie's car. Jimmy and Sally get out, greeting George and Jeannie and wishing George a happy birthday. Sally awkwardly reaches into the backseat. She gives George a birthday pie.

"It's strawberry rhubarb," she says. "Fresh baked today."

"Strawberry rhubarb. My favorite."

George hugs Sally and gives her a peck on the cheek.

"Sal, you are the best pie maker I know. And I know we will enjoy this. Thanks so much," he says. "I know that every year you make me something, and every year I say 'You don't have to do it.' But the truth is I always look forward to Sally's birthday special."

George takes a quick peek at the pie and then puts it in the car.

"You guys look sharp tonight," Jeannie remarks. "It's nice to see you dressed up for a change."

"I got this sport coat when I got out of the Army," Jimmy says. "It still fits, a little tight but still fits."

"I don't mind the jacket, but the tie I could do without," George chimes in.

They start walking toward the door.

"What about us?" Sally says, gesturing to Jeannie. "Don't we count?"

"You two always look nice," Jimmy says. "You'll be the best-looking women at the wake."

"But why don't you ever tell us that?" Sally says as they walk.

"I tell you how nice you look all the time," Jimmy says.

"You tell me how sexy I look," Sally says, "and that just means you're horn–"

"Saying you're sexy is the same thing," Jimmy interrupts. "Don't you like it?"

George points toward the front door.

"Isn't that Tommy?" he says. "And who's that with him?"

"Could be his sister," Jeannie says.

"No, his sister's taller than that," Sally points out.

"Where?" asks Jimmy, "All I see is a group of guys smoking."

"Not by the door," George replies. "At the top of the steps."

As they approach the steps, they confirm that it is Tommy. Tommy's an old friend from when they all—Jimmy, George, Big Butch, and Tommy—worked at Bob's Beef Burgers. They flipped hamburgers part-time for a couple years during high school. Tommy is tall. He looks like one of the Righteous Brothers with his hair always perfect. He stands at the top of the steps with his left hand in his pocket and his right hand holds a cigarette tight to his lips, as if he is nervously waiting. When they get close enough, Tommy introduces everyone to his friend, Rosemary. Jimmy holds the door. Everyone enters the funeral home. Sally pulls Jimmy's coat sleeve.

"I can't believe he brought a date to a funeral," she whispers.

Jimmy leans down.

"I can't either," he whispers back. "This is freakin' weird."

The atmosphere was the usual solemnity that you expect in a funeral home. A bald-headed man in a dark gray suit and maroon tie directs them to sign the registry. Sally and Jeannie sign the book, and then Tommy. The bald-headed man introduces himself.

"I'm John Collins, the assistant director."

Then, he asks how they knew the deceased. Jimmy speaks, saying that they were all good friends. Tommy, standing in the back, looks directly at the funeral director and gestures a big nod. The director then asks the group to follow him.

They walk down the hall just a little way and the director opens the door and motions for them to step in. Tommy and his date, Rosemary go first, then George and Jeannie, with Jimmy, and Sally last.

They cannot believe their eyes. It's like a party. People standing with drinks in their hands, talking and laughing. Jimmy and Sally, George and Jeannie all look at each other, amazed and confused. The only one who speaks is Jimmy.

"What the fuck is this?" he asks.

Tommy is surprised, but not too surprised, and hustles them to the keg of beer, where he taps everybody a glass.

"What the fuck is this?" Jimmy continues to say.

George is silent with question marks in his eyes. Sally and Jeannie look around with their mouths open.

"This is weird," the women whisper to each other.

George recognizes people from his past. He knows more people at this funeral than he expected.

Organ music begins, lights dim, and people hush. The wall opposite the entrance of the room slides slowly out of sight, revealing, in the middle of the floor, Big Butch in his coffin. A spotlight shines upon him and the organ music stops. It grows quiet, too quiet.

The next moment seems like an hour, no one speaks a word, not a muscle moves. Everyone is gripped in total suspension staring at Big Butch in his coffin. Without warning, the organ resumes and everyone is jolted back.

The ghostly music is a familiar song, the song of Happy Birthday, slowed to a spooky pace. Without the four of them knowing, the people around them take a couple of steps back, leaving George and Jeannie, Jimmy and Sally in a spotlight of their own. The spotlight shining on Big Butch changes to an eerie blue color and very slowly Big Butch sits up in his coffin.

"Oh my God!" Jeannie gasps.

She grabs George.

"Holy shit!" Sally yells.

She hangs on Jimmy's arm.

Big Butch, now sitting straight up in the coffin, stares at George. Slowly, he raises his arm and points his finger at George. The organ starts to play at the normal tempo. All the people join the organ and sing the Happy Birthday song, ending with a loud, "happy birthday, dear George, happy birthday to you!"

Clapping and cheering fills the room. From the speakers, they hear the unmistakable opening of the Beatles "Birthday." Psychedelic Willy runs out with a microphone in hand, dressed in a red Sergeant Pepper uniform and singing.

People start to clap and cheer. Willy encourages everyone to sing along. Everyone starts to sing along and groove. Jimmy is too stunned to join in and too shocked to drink his beer.

George drops his head and gives a slight shake "no."

"Can you believe this? George, this is unbelievable," Jeannie says.

Jeannie grabs George by the arm.

"Happy birthday, I love you," she says.

Jimmy and Sally recede from the spotlight and go to the side of the room. They survey the room, then look at each other, look around some more, then look at each other, and then gaze around the room again. Amidst the loud singing, Jimmy leans over to Sally's ear.

"I can't fuckin' believe this," Jimmy says. "This is so wild. How did they do all this without us knowing?"

Sally tugs on Jimmy's sleeve. Jimmy tilts slightly.

"I guess it was such a great secret, they didn't want everyone to know," she says.

Jimmy nods "yes." Finally, the singing ends, and the clapping and cheering ends. People gather around George and Jeannie, giving congratulations.

They all keep asking the same stupid question, "Were you surprised?"

"It seems like everybody knew that Big Butch wasn't dead," Jimmy says to Sally. "And it was a freakin' party for George."

"Yeah, it does seem that way," Sally says.

"Everyone knew. Except us," Jimmy says. "All week long I was in fucking mourning. Grieving for an asshole sitting in a coffin."

Sally sighs. Sally knows that Jimmy's hurt and pissed off.

"Jimmy, you're George's best friend. They didn't want you to slip up," she says.

Jimmy goes to Big Butch. Other guests help him out of the coffin. Big Butch, now standing, shakes Jimmy's hand. Jimmy offers a fake smile meant to lure Butch into his confidence.

"This was fuckin' wild. I can't believe you did this," Jimmy says. "How did you come up with this idea?"

Big Butch smiles.

"I was just a prop," Butch says. "Willy is the man behind the whole thing. It was his idea and he put the whole thing together."

"You mean, Psychedelic Willy thought this up and put it all together? You mean like getting the funeral home and sending out invitations?"

"Yeah. He took care of everything. All I had to do was hide in my house for three days."

"You didn't go to work?" Jimmy asks.

"No. I took vacation," Butch explains. "I worked on my basement a little bit. Sat around watching TV and read. It was pretty neat."

"You didn't go out of your house for three days?"

"No," Butch says.

"You were sitting at home watching 'Chico and the Man,' 'Rockford Files,' and working on your basement," Jimmy says, "while I'm crying in my beer because one of my best friends is dead! Don't you think that's being a fucking prick?"

"Yeah, you're right. I never thought about that," Butch says. "All I thought about was how cool a surprise it would be for George. I never thought that it would get you upset. I did what Willy told me to do."

Butch looks at Jimmy.

"I'm sorry, Jimmy, I never wanted to put you through that shit," he says.

For a moment, Jimmy doesn't say anything, then he makes a frown that causes his mustache to droop down and nods. Suddenly, he has a thought.

"How did you get here?" Jimmy asks.

"Willy picked me up in the hearse. He made me lie in the back, that way nobody would see me. And if they did, I was in a hearse, and I would get used to being dead," Butch says. "Willy starts playing 'Stairway to Heaven.'"

Big Butch laughs.

"Willy is fucking crazy," he adds. "He had the funeral home put this makeup on me. It was really creepy in the coffin. I couldn't wait to get out."

"You sure as hell made a really good dead guy," Jimmy says.

"That's because I didn't have to do anything but lay in a coffin."

"So, when did Willy come up with this idea?"

"About two months ago. It was a Saturday afternoon, raining like hell, I hear a knock on the back door. I look out and there's Willy standing there in a yellow slicker looking like a New England fisherman, with his shit eating grin. He walked over."

"He walked over!" Jimmy exclaims. "From his house? That's about two miles or so."

"Yeah. He said walking in the rain helped clear his thoughts. And that's when he came up with the idea of this crazy birthday party."

Jimmy stares at Big Butch and squints with curiosity, but inside he is starting to boil.

"He came up with this whole idea by walking in the rain?" Jimmy asks.

"Yeah, we were sitting at the kitchen table, having coffee, and smoking a little herb and Willy starts telling me about his idea," Butch says. "He asked me for paper and pencil, which I give to him, and he starts writing this whole thing down. He's writing it down like it's a play or a TV show. He is writing down footnotes about the undertaker, the music, and whatnot. I just sat there and watched Willy getting, like, overwhelmed with excitement. All this crazy creativity just poured out of him. And it turned out exactly how he planned it."

"Who else knew about it?"

"Me. I told my mom and dad, just in case anybody would say something about me dying. Willy invited people, telling them it was a surprise birthday party held at the funeral home. I don't think anybody knew about the details but me."

Big Butch pats Jimmy on the shoulder.

"You did your part by being you," Butch says. "If you wouldn't have been you, it wouldn't have been right to George."

Big Butch smiles.

"You played your part perfect," Butch says.

Jimmy doesn't quite understand, but he smiles and raises his beer as to give a toast. Without thinking, the words just come out.

"A job well done," Jimmy says.

He walks back to Sally. Jimmy wants to talk to Willy. He has a hard time faking that he is here for George and Jeannie, faking that he is enjoying the party, faking that he is here with Sally, carefree. He wants to. He wishes he could. But he's stuck sorting what's inside himself — and once more he is disappointed in himself.

Jimmy has the feeling that no one trusts him. Or maybe no one thinks they can rely on him. Jimmy worries that he's a joke and a bad one at that. Jimmy sometimes feels that way at work and sometimes feels that way when he is alone. He seldom feels that way with Sally.

Jimmy turns to her and takes her hand. Sally peers at Jimmy's face and she seems to read him.

"Some party," she says flatly.

Jimmy nods. Sally reaches to him and kisses him on the cheek. Jimmy squeezes her hand. Jimmy feels a different hand on his shoulder. When he turns, there is Cheesy with his big "cheesy" smile, Hawaiian shirt, and his wife, Martha, at his side.

"Cheese, what the hell are you doing here? You usually don't come home 'til August," Jimmy asks.

"Willy gave me a call, when I heard about Big Butch laying in a coffin and all that shit," he says. "I just couldn't miss this. You guys know Martha."

Jimmy and Sally nod.

"Oh, sure," Jimmy says.

Willy slides in front of them, wearing his red Sergeant Pepper out-
fit and staying in character as if he is one of the Beatles. He would have
to be Paul or John.

"Are you having a smashing time?" Willy asks with his fake British
accent.

Sally responds, "Oh, this is really great."

Jimmy just raises his glass of beer. Willy rambles about how much
fun it was driving the hearse with Big Butch in the back and having
the undertaker put makeup on him and Big Butch. He beams with
pride with the fact that everything went so well and that everyone
could keep a secret.

Jimmy drops Sally's hand and steps closer to Willy. With a serious
stare, Jimmy blurts out the words that he has tried to conceal.

"Why didn't you tell me about the party?" he asks.

Willy glances down and clears his throat.

"It was best that you didn't know," he says without hesitation. "It
was more natural. It was the way it was supposed to be."

Jimmy stands before Willy, his arms folded as he tries to conceal
his anger. Jimmy looks into Willy's eyes.

"I don't get it, Willy."

"Damn, Jimmy. What don't you get?" Willy says. "It was better
that you didn't know."

"It was perfect that you didn't know," Cheesy chimes in. "No
chance of George getting wise."

Jimmy looks at Willy.

"That's it? No other reason?"

"Well," says Willy, "there is the fact that you can't keep a secret
when you're drunk."

Jimmy's voice goes up an octave and gets louder.

"So, you didn't tell me because I'm a drunk," he snaps.

"I'm not saying that," Willy spouts back. "It was better that
you didn't know, because then you would act more natural around
George."

Jimmy nods and sips his beer. Sally tugs on Jimmy's arm.

"Jimmy, I think it's time."

"Time for what?" Jimmy snarls.

Sally rolls her eyes, holding her stomach and with a sneer of
annoyance.

"The baby, the baby," she says with excitement rising in her voice.

"The baby? Oh, the baby!" he says. "Are you all right? Are you sure it's time?"

"Yes. I'm sure," Sally says, with tears building in her eyes. "It's time to go."

Jimmy hands Willy his beer.

"We got to go," Jimmy says.

Willy stands there looking more confused than normal.

"Oh, man, Sally,' Cheesy says. "Are you having your baby?"

Sally nods. Martha asks if there's anything she can do. With uncertainty on Sally's face, she tells her she didn't think so, that she should make it to the hospital. Jimmy supports Sally with his arm. He motions for Jeannie to come over and tells her it's time for the baby.

"Oh, my God! Time for the baby," Jeannie exclaims.

Jeannie helps Jimmy escort Sally to the car and assists her into the Mustang.

"Tell everybody it was a great party and wish George a happy birthday..." Jimmy says as he takes the wheel.

"Jimmy, you don't have a driver's license," Jeannie shouts.

"So, fucking what?" he replies. "I'm driving my wife to the hospital."

Sally waves to Jeannie and tells her that she is fine and things will be okay. Jeannie waves back. "Good luck," Jeannie calls, "and we'll be praying for you."

As they speed off, Jimmy asks if the pains are great.

"Yes, I'm having pain."

Sally is unusually quiet.

"Do you...do you..." Jimmy stutters, "do you think your water is going to break?"

"Of course, it will break," Sally replies, "but I don't know when. Why are you asking me these questions?"

Jimmy thinks about it.

"I guess to keep your mind off it," he says. "I don't know. To help us relax."

"Well, it's not working," Sally mutters.

"I hope your water don't break in the car."

"For Christ's sake Jimmy, is that all you think about, is this damn car!"

"No. No," he says. "I'm just thinking it will be messy for you."

"Jimmy, drive the freakin' car."

"Should I turn on the radio?" he asks.

"No. Just drive to the hospital."

They pull into the emergency entrance. Jimmy stops the car and hops out as if he were in an action-adventure television program.

"My wife's having a baby," he yells. "My wife's having a baby."

He repeats this over and over, dashing into the emergency room. Once he's in the building, he freezes with fear.

"My wife is having a baby," he keeps announcing.

Two nurses grab a gurney. They ask where she is. Jimmy points to the door.

"In the car," he shouts. "In the car!"

The nurses run out and Jimmy follows. Behind the open passenger door, Sally now sits on the edge of the bucket seat with her feet on the street, the tears now on her cheeks.

"Oh no, my water broke," she mutters.

The nurses whisk Sally onto the stretcher and roll off at what seemed like a reckless speed. Jimmy pulls the car into a proper parking space and hurries back inside. When he arrives at the delivery room, the doctor and the nurses all smile with reassurance and calm. Sally scoots onto the table and Jimmy puts on the gown. As they position everything for delivery, Jimmy stands in silence.

All he can think is… another kid! A baby!

Nurses urge Jimmy to hold Sally's hand and coach her on breathing techniques. Jimmy's excitement keeps him from remembering anything that he learned from those silly classes that Sally made him take. Sally squeezes his hand, and Jimmy sees her face and hears her pain.

Jimmy's mind echoes, only a half hour ago he was angry at Willy at this crazy party in a funeral home drinking a beer. Now he stands in this chilly room with his heart pounding. He stares at Sally. The numbness washes away. He's in the moment. Jimmy leans very close to Sally.

There is beer on his breath.

"You can do it, Sal," he says. "Sally, everything is going to be okay."

Sally closes her eyes for a moment.

"It sounds like you're cheering on a baseball player," she says to him.

Sally opens her eyes. She smiles at him.

"Jimmy, it's all going to be okay," she tells him.

From then on, Jimmy only hears nurses say, "pant, pant" and "push, push."

A big push.

"Okay, we can see the baby now," the doctor says.

Jimmy moves down to see the arrival. Sally exhales. With a pain-filled moan from Sally, a cry fills the room. Jimmy gazes at their squirming, sticky newborn baby.

"Oh, he's beautiful," Jimmy says.

The doctor corrects him.

"No, sir, she is beautiful."

Jimmy looks upon Sally.

With great enthusiasm and gratitude, he says, "Sally, it's a girl. We had a girl."

Sally smiles with happy tears in her eyes.

"It's a girl," she says. "You were right, Jimmy."

Jimmy cuts his daughter's cord. The nurses wipe off the new arrival. Sally holds her newborn with love and pride. Sally squeezes Jimmy's hand with the baby in her other arm.

"She is beautiful," Sally agrees.

After the nurses make sure that Sally and the baby are healthy and stable, the family moves to a room. Sally nurses the newborn for the first time.

"We need to give her a name, Sal," Jimmy says. "If she were a boy, we could name him George. You know, being born on George's birthday and all."

Sally laughs.

"We can name her Georgia," she suggests with joyful play in her voice.

Jimmy nods.

"That's a good name, Georgia Washburn," he says after thinking about it. "That sounds pretty neat."

"Jimmy, I was just kidding!" Sally protests. "Georgia Washburn! Kids would start calling her George Washington."

"No, they wouldn't," he says. "I like our name Washburn. We could call her Georgia Jean."

"Georgia Jean Washburn," Sally repeats, and he could tell she was seriously considering it, "sounds like a lawyer or a writer...or something like that."

"That's good, Sal," Jimmy says. "We need a lawyer in the family."

"Georgia Jean is kind of cute," she says.

"She would already have a song by Ray Charles," he says.

He keeps listing reasons Georgia Jean is a good name.

"George and Jeannie would really be surprised," he says.

"But then if they had a girl, they would feel obligated to call her, Jimmie Sal," Sally points out. "Spelling it with an I-E."

"No, they wouldn't," Jimmy insists. "I like it…. Georgia Jean."

Sally smiles.

"Okay, Jimmy. Georgia Jean."

Jimmy kisses Sally gently, telling her that she did a fantastic job. That he will tell the whole story to her mom and call his mom once more tonight, but nobody else until tomorrow. Now he will leave her and Georgia Jean to get a good night's sleep. Sally holds Jimmy's hand tighter.

"Jimmy, you are going home?" Sally says. "I mean you're not going to–"

Jimmy puts his hand up, stopping her.

"I am not going out drinking to celebrate the birth of our daughter," he promises. "Besides your mom is still at the house watching Little Jimmy. I got to get there soon or she'll call the cops."

Sally motions for him to come closer. They kiss.

"Be careful driving home," Sally whispers to him, "you don't want to get stopped, with no license and all."

Jimmy kisses Sally again.

"I'll be extra careful," he says, "and besides I have Georgia Jean looking out for me too."

They kiss good night a final time.

Saturday, May 25, 1974

The phone rings.

Jimmy answers, "Yeah? Hello?"

Sally's voice greets him.

"Jimmy?"

"Sally, are you okay? Is the baby okay?" he asks. "What time is it?"

"Early," Sally replies. "About 6:15."

On the other end of the phone, Sally explains that everything's fine. She just finished feeding the baby and she is homesick. She wonders what Little Jimmy will think about his new baby sister.

"It will be quite a treat for Little Jimmy to go to the hospital and meet his little sister," Jimmy says. "What time do you want us to come?"

"Oh, come soon. I miss you guys," Sally says without hesitation.

"Okay."

They end the phone call with a blown kiss, and "I love you."

Jimmy puts on his pants, a T-shirt, and hustles to the kitchen. He lights a cigarette and makes coffee. He looks at the clock, 6:30, and he thinks Little Jimmy should be up soon. He also wonders if it's too early to call his mother and ask her for a ride to the hospital. He sits at the kitchen table, tapping his cigarette in the ashtray, and staring at the coffee pot. Waiting is not one of Jimmy's good qualities.

His head swims with thoughts as he tries to plan the day. His mind jumps from Sally and the baby, to calling Sally's mom, to calling Jeannie and George, to buying that Falcon station wagon from Willy's grandfather. He really wants to surprise Sally.

Jimmy sighs. He sits with his elbows on the table and his head in his hands.

"I have all this shit to do and I'm sitting here watching a freaking coffee pot," he says out loud to himself. "I want my brain to slow down."

And in all this thinking, there is the underlying thought, his true goal…that he would be sitting on the barstool at the end of the day telling his fantastic Jimmy story to whoever would listen. It is the start of the day, but in Jimmy's world, he longs to reach the end.

He considers going back to bed and letting Little Jimmy wake him. Then Jimmy hears his mother's voice in his head.

"Jimmy, you have two speeds. Stop and fast, there's nothing in between."

He sits back in his chair and sighs again. In a prayer that was more like a hope or a wish, he asks if he could get done what he wanted to do today. Then, Jimmy recognizes the bump-thump, bump-thump of Little Jimmy on the stairs. Jimmy smiles a smile he could never fake. His day is off to a loving start.

Jimmy calls his mother, hating the fact that he doesn't have a driver's license and now depends on somebody else. She graciously takes him and Little Jimmy, with a bouquet of flowers, to the hospital. Little Jimmy is amazed at the hospital and the nurses, and at seeing his little baby sister through a glass window. Little Jimmy presses himself against the glass.

"Georgia Jean," Little Jimmy says for the first time.

Little Jimmy is only allowed in the hallway where you view the babies. So, Sally sneaks out of her room and walks very slowly toward her visitors.

"Hello," she says quietly.

Little Jimmy turns.

"Mommy!" he yells.

He runs down the hall. The sound of the pat, pat, pat of his two-and-a-half-year-old feet alarms the strict nurse. She points her finger and scolds everyone for not obeying the rules. As she is shushing Sally into her room, Jimmy picks up Little Jimmy and takes him back to the big glass window in front of the babies. His mother, Eleanor, reassures him that she'll take care of Little Jimmy and urges him to go into Sally's room with the flowers.

Sally tells him that she and the baby will come home Monday or Tuesday and that she is incredibly relieved that the baby's room is all set up. Jimmy tells her of all the people he called and their reactions to the baby. Sally asks what Jeannie and George said about naming her Georgia Jean?

"Oh, they loved it, especially George. He said, 'Wow, my name-sake is a girl' and he laughed. But it was a good laugh. Jeannie was really pleased that her name was included."

Sally knows that Jimmy loves telling the story of how Georgia Jean arrived into the world. She also knows according to who he's talking to the story will change a bit. But she loves that part of him.

As Jimmy talks of his busy day, they hold hands and Sally allows tears to roll down her cheeks again.

"What's wrong?" Jimmy asks immediately.

Sally wipes her eyes.

"I don't know," she admits. "I'm happy and frightened at the same time."

Jimmy feels puzzled.

"I don't understand," he says. "What are you frightened of?"

"You know, responsibility," she says. "Having two kids at the same time. Being Supermom. Maybe not doing it right."

"Sal, you're a great mom," he reassures her. "There's nothing to be afraid of."

"I guess my biggest fear is about your—"

The phone by the bed rings. It interrupts Sally. Jimmy picks it up.

"Hello?" he answers.

Jeannie greets him.

"Oh, hi, Jeannie," he says. "Yes, everything's great. Here's Sally."

As Jimmy hands her the phone, Sally shakes her head with disappointment. She gives Jimmy a look that says he got out of this one. Jimmy realizes that it's his cue to leave. He leans over and kisses Sally on the cheek, telling her that Little Jimmy's getting antsy with his mother and it's best that they leave. He'll call her later, once again he kisses her on the cheek.

"I love you," he says as he walks out.

On the way home, Jimmy's mom agrees to keep Little Jimmy overnight. Tomorrow morning, she will pick up Jimmy and take them both to the hospital. Eleanor knows when to help and when not to help. Jimmy called Willy from the hospital about the Falcon station wagon and now Willy's waiting for him when Eleanor pulls up in front of Jimmy's house.

Willy comes to Eleanor's car and says hello to Eleanor and Little Jimmy. Jimmy kisses Little Jimmy and tells him to "be a good boy for Grandma" and kisses and thanks his mom. Eleanor and Little Jimmy leave.

"You sure got a nice mom," Willy says.

"Yeah, she has been a good mom to me," Jimmy says. "I wouldn't put up with the crap that I pulled."

"I guess that's true for most of us," Willy says. "So you got a new kid, a little girl. Far out, two kids."

"Yeah, it was pretty crazy going to Big Butch's funeral, that wasn't a funeral, and then Sal going into labor. I thought for sure that she was going to have the baby in the car."

Jimmy takes a deep breath. He folds his arms, restricting his body language. He shifts his weight so that he is leaning on his right leg.

"Do you realize that you put me through a bunch of shit?" Jimmy blurts out. "For four days I was grieving the loss of a close friend, thinking that he was dead."

Willy puts his hands up and shrugs his shoulders.

"Yes and No. I knew that you would be freaking out, but I didn't think like, really freaking out," Willy admits. "Oh man, it was such a great gag. George was so freakin' surprised, and George was the perfect person to do it to. You, of all people, know how George is so laid back and unassuming. I didn't mean to get you all fucked up about this. I thought you, being George's best friend, would laugh your ass off. It was fuckin' funny, man."

Jimmy starts to breathe. He brings his arms to his sides. He nods.

"I got to admit it was funny and I know George did have a great time, and you did one hell of a job, Willy. I just wish that I knew about it."

Willy puts out his hand for Jimmy to shake.

"I was just thinking about the surprise and nothing else. Sorry, man."

Out of politeness, Jimmy shakes his hand. He has no idea what to say.

"Listen, my grandfather said he'll take $600 for the Falcon," says Willy.

Jimmy is relieved that the subject has changed.

"It's turquoise. Not a metallic turquoise, straight plain turquoise," Willy says. "It runs good, it's inspected and the radio works. Oh, the tires are new, too."

"Sounds perfect," Jimmy says. "I got the money upstairs. You think we can make a deal today?"

"Yeah, Grandpa is up for it," Willy says.

Jimmy retrieves the money and finds Willy leaning against his 1958 Willys Jeep Utility Wagon, smoking a cigarette. Jimmy, as well as most people, get a kick out of Willy driving a Willys Jeep. Willy opens the door.

"Hop in."

Before Jimmy can move, Willy spouts out, "Oh, Shit. I need to make room for you."

With one arm and one swoop, some debris is pushed to the floor.

"Okay, hop in," Willy says again.

Jimmy stares at the floor, littered with McDonald's bags, Yocco's hot dog wrappers, and red and white Marlboro cigarette packs.

"Willy, don't you ever clean out your Jeep?" barks Jimmy, "This is freakin' disgusting. This could be a really cool vehicle. It's a classic, for Christ's sake."

Willy slides in behind the steering wheel.

"Stop being so full of yourself and get in the car. I like this Jeep just the way it is, with dull green paint and all," he says. "People see this old Willys and they think, 'now that guy don't give a shit' and they're right."

"This dull green is called 'Glenwood Green' and with new paint, it would look kick ass," Jimmy banters back.

Something catches Jimmy's eye.

"Hey, what's that in the back?" he asks.

Willy glances in the rear-view mirror.

"Oh, that's an old Philco floor model radio," Willy answers. "I got it from my Uncle Leonard."

"Does it work?"

"I don't know. I just got it the other day."

As Willy drives, he keeps saying how nice the Falcon is and that his grandfather is such a nut about his car.

Willy laughs and says, "What a waste of time."

Jimmy looks at Willy and confirms what he always knew, that Willy really doesn't give a shit.

At Willy's grandfather's house, the station wagon is all washed, shined, and even the interior is spotless. Willy's grandfather is medium height, medium build, with a kind face, and a head full of thick gray hair. His clothing is a bit disheveled. Willy introduces Jimmy.

"This is Grandpa Bill," he says.

"Oh, you are a William," Jimmy says. "That's where Willy gets his name?"

"Yeah, he's actually Willy the Third," Grandpa Bill says.

Jimmy laughs with a devilish glance to Willy.

"Willy the Third," Jimmy repeats. "Sounds pretty cool to me."

"That's enough of that shit," Psychedelic Willy says.

Grandpa Bill opens the hood with pride. To Jimmy's amazement, the engine is clean and gleaming like a new car.

"I wipe her off every night. Just use the dry rag, but if you do it from brand-new, it's really no trouble at all," Grandpa Bills explains. "She still runs good, even though she's ten-years-old. I changed the oil regular and I put new brakes and tires on her last year."

"Willy was right, you sure took good care of her," Jimmy says. "I'll take her."

On the way over to the notary, Grandpa Bill tells them stories about driving cross country in the 1920s on a motorcycle, but he says "motor-sickle." He talks about the jobs he had during the Depression. As Grandpa Bill put it, "I finally got my ass out of a gin mill and started to live doing things that I only thought about when sitting on a bar stool."

Jimmy could see the roots of Willy's family tree of wide-range thinking.

At the notary, life offers a slap in the face. Jimmy's surprise gift for Sally is not working out. Having no license, he can't prove who he is. The insurance cost is high because of his DUI. It makes more sense to put the car in Sally's name.

Having Willy and his grandfather there is a waste of their time. They witness his embarrassment. It puts Jimmy in a longing mood for his barstool at Bucky's place. Jimmy has just started to get over not knowing about George's surprise party. Now Willy can see and feel more of the shame that Jimmy carries.

"I hate that I put you through this. Just take me home," says Jimmy.

On the way home, Jimmy doesn't say much of anything and feels lucky that Grandpa Bill does all the talking. Willy and his grandfather offer a good solution. They'll park the Falcon station wagon in front of Jimmy's house. That way when Sally comes home from the hospital, she will see it and be surprised. When Sally is ready, she can go to the notary and have it put in her name. The solution perks Jimmy up, but still does not take away the deep embarrassment of the consequences caused by his drinking.

Despite his humiliation, Jimmy thanks Willy and Grandpa Bill for doing all this for him. Willy shakes Jimmy's hand.

"It's okay," Willy says, "you deserve it."

By this time, it is past four o'clock in the afternoon and Jimmy heads up the hill to Bucky's place. As he trudges to his favorite perch, Willy's words dominate his thoughts.

"It's okay, you deserve it."

What do I deserve? Why do I deserve it? What did Willy mean? The thoughts repeat in his brain. Feelings of mistrust jab at the bitterness toward Willy. Jimmy didn't like it, nor did he want to be pissed off with Willy. But emotions churn constantly in Jimmy, pointing the finger at Willy for not telling him about the surprise party. After all, George is his best friend. And Grandpa Bill talking about getting his ass out of a gin mill. Jimmy needs this anger. He needs to be upset so he can drink without guilt.

Stanley is at his regular spot. When Jimmy glides onto the barstool next to him, Stanley smiles.

"How was Big Butch's funeral?" Stanley asks.

Jimmy raises his eyebrows.

"There was no fucking funeral," Jimmy says. "It ended up being a surprise birthday party for George."

"A surprise birthday party at a funeral home?" Stanley spouts.

"Yeah, it was really wild," Jimmy says. "But the best news is that Sally had a baby girl. Georgia Jean, seven-and-a-half pounds, 22 inches long. Here, have a cigar."

"That is grand! Now you have a boy and a girl. Wonderful."

As Jimmy hands Stanley the cigar, Stanley puts his hand up.

"No thanks," he says. "You know I don't smoke."

Jimmy smiles.

"But Evie does," he says. "Give it to her."

"Okay, Jimmy," Stanley says, accepting the cigar and putting it in his shirt pocket. "I think she'll get a kick out of it. Where did you get cigars? "

"When we were shopping at Ernie's Market, went across the street to Hillside Pharmacy and got a box of El Producto the cigar that George Burns smokes," Jimmy explains.

Stanley grins.

"I'll make sure that I tell Evie that," he says.

Haasie sets a beer in front of Jimmy.

"Here Haasie, have a cigar," Jimmy announces. "It's a girl!"

Haasie reaches for the Corby's whiskey bottle and three shot glasses and says, "This calls for a toast. On the house."

Stanley says, "None for me, I'll toast with my beer."

"Come on, Stanley," Jimmy says. "You can have a shot."

"No disrespect to your daughter," Stanley says, "but it's past 4:30 and I must be going soon."

He tells of having plans, and insists that he will toast with his beer. Haasie looks at Jimmy and nods okay. Haasie raises a shot glass and asks Jimmy what his daughter's name is.

"Georgia Jean," Jimmy proudly replies.

They all raise their glasses and toast.

"To Georgia Jean. May she be happy and healthy."

Haasie tells Jimmy "congratulations," sets up two more beers, and goes about his work.

Stanley turns to Jimmy.

"Georgia Jean, that's a beautiful name," he says. "How did you pick that?"

"We named her after my friend, George, and his wife, Jeannie. She was born on George's birthday, so we thought it would be neat."

"A little girl," Stanley says. "You must have everything around the house in pink. Evie and I only had our son, Harry."

Jimmy looks confused but doesn't say anything.

"We named him Harry because my father was named Harry and because Evie's father was named Harry," Stanley says. "It was a pretty safe bet, naming him Harry."

"Harry is a good name," Jimmy agrees.

"He died in Korea twenty years ago," Stanley says. "We would love to have grandchildren. You are so lucky to have these children, Jimmy."

"I'm sorry about your son," Jimmy says. "Never knew that."

"It happened a long time ago," Stanley says, holding up his beer again. "Today is a celebration of life. So, tell me, is Sally okay and the baby okay? How's Little Jimmy taking the new addition?"

"Everything's fine. We almost didn't make it to the hospital," Jimmy says. "We were at the party, the viewing for the death of Big Butch, when Sally said to me, 'It's time' and I said 'Time for what?' 'The baby, the baby,' she tells me. I said the hell with it. I'm driving my wife to the hospital and off we go to the hospital. Her water broke as we arrived, they put her on a stretcher, and off to the delivery room. Next thing you know I'm in a surgical gown coaching Sally on her breathing and then with a cry, Georgia Jean is saying hello to the world. Everything happened so fast. It really was amazing. Little Jimmy is so excited about having a little sister."

"I'm glad everything worked out fine," Stanley says. "Now you have more responsibility, Jimmy."

"Yeah, I know," he says. "I need to do better."

"In what way?" asks Stanley.

"I don't know," Jimmy says. "My job is pretty secure, and Uncle Jack treats me right as far as money goes. I have this feeling that I should do something more."

"Maybe you should do something less and that way you could do more," Stanley suggests.

"What the fuck exactly does that mean?" Jimmy says.

"Think about it. What could you do less of that would give you more?"

"You're talking in fucking riddles, Stanley."

Jimmy pulls his elbows off the bar and straightens up on his stool. He sips his beer. He could see himself in the back-bar mirror. And for some reason, he takes a good look at himself. He sees himself sitting on the barstool drinking his beer, as if it were the first time he observed himself. Then the light bulb goes on in Jimmy's brain, deep inside. He knows exactly what Stanley is talking about.

Jimmy looks at Stanley.

"I get it," Jimmy says. "If I drink less, I'll get more… More what?"

Stanley smiles.

"More everything," the old man says.

"What about you?" Jimmy says. "You're sitting at the bar just like me. You drink."

"Yes, I drink. And I enjoy drinking. I enjoy your company for the hour or two that we spend together in the bar. I go home," Stanley explains. "You stay. The Jimmy that emerges later on, I would not enjoy."

Stanley pauses.

"You know, Jimmy, we could sit and have a cup of coffee in my shop and still talk about the things that we talk about in a bar. I would enjoy that just as much."

Jimmy looks at himself once more in the mirror. He watches himself sip his beer and he sips his beer again. His eyes fall to the bar and he turns his head towards Stanley.

"I was thinking it was all about dying, that change was dying," Jimmy says, "but change is all about being born."

Thank you

… to all my friends and family that urged and inspired me to travel the road of creativity

… to the Lehigh Valley Storytelling Guild for a firm foundation in storytelling

A special thanks to Angel Ackerman and the crew at Parisian Phoenix Publishing for doing what I could have never done.

ALSO BY LARRY SCEURMAN

Coffee in the Morning, coming 2023
> A collection of short stories that come from truth, dreams
> and fabrication

Mr. Albert in the House of Penquins, late 2023
> Private Investigator Peter Hawkins, after receiving a summons
> to appear as the star witness before a grand jury, hides in a
> convent. What he learns about himself in his time among the
> sisters and the staff changes his destiny.

Larry Sceurman grew up in the Kaywin section of Bethlehem, Pa., in the 1950s and 1960s.

In his early teens, he worked with his grandfather in a small auto body repair shop where he observed that stories were a big part of the human experience. From vocational teacher to storyteller and now author, Larry has learned and shared the value of stories. He mixes truth and fiction to produce enjoyable, thought-provoking snippets of life.

Larry is influenced by the writings of Laura E. Richards, John O'Connor, Richard Ford, Michael J. Meade, Richard Rohr, and Billy Collins.

Also from Parisian Phoenix Publishing

FICTION:
By Angel Ackerman:
"The Fashion and Fiends" Series
    Manipulations
    Courting Apparitions
    Recovery
    Road Trip coming in 2023
Not the Quiet French Kid

Trapped by Seneca Blue; photos by Joan Zachary

POETRY:
TWISTS: Gathered Ephemera by darrell parry

NON-FICTION:
Stops Along The Way by Charles Ticho

Not an Able-Bodied White Man with Money: Expressions of Alternative Perspectives Influenced by Experiences in Lehigh Valley, Pennsylvania. Edited by Angel R. Ackerman

Peruse and purchase all our titles at online retailers
or order thru your favorite independent bookseller.

PUBLISHER'S NOTE

Larry Sceurman and I started work together on what we thought would be an anthology of stories called, *Coffee in the Morning*. But as I read the stories, I realized Larry had more to offer. And once I read *The Death of Big Butch*, I knew it had the power to stand as its own novella.

This is Larry's debut work in print. He's been a storyteller for years, but different reasons kept him from publishing until…one fateful weekend in June when I accompanied our photographer Joan Zachary to a Greater Lehigh Valley Writers' Group meeting where she gave a talk on the inspirational power of photography and how original photography can improve your book.

Larry sent me a submission. And Big Butch hit home. The main character in the story is Jimmy Washburn, an auto body technician from a small Pennsylvanian town. The story takes place in May 1974. He has a son he calls Little Jimmy.

My dad was Jimmy Ackerman and he was a diesel mechanic in a small Pennsylvanian town. My brother was also Little Jimmy. And I was born in May 1975. My dad, like Jimmy Washburn, spent a lot of time with other men in bars like the one Jimmy drinks in, and the other men in Larry's story are men with names like

Cheesy (also my first dog's name) and Butch (my mother's partner for probably the last 15 years).

My daughter posed for the cover photo of this novella, and one of the outtakes features Larry coaching Eva on what he wants to see in the scene. But the photo Joan captures of that moment, well, it says so much more.

I asked Eva what Larry said to her to make her look so pensive and a little sad. She said Larry reminded her of our Butch, and she hadn't expected that, and that she missed our Butch.

My mother's neighbor, whom we call Grandma, texted me later that night and said our Butch was not well. I reached out to my mother to see if Eva could see our Butch.

But my mother replied that our Butch had died that night.

My daughter considered Butch a grandfather figure in her life, so I asked Larry if I could memorialize our Butch in a page in the back of his book with that photo. So here it is.

Our Butch was a man of many tattoos and a fluffy beard, distributing Yoo-Hoo and driving Eva around in the bucket of the tractor. And Eva will miss him.

~Angel Ackerman